First Published by Aspects Publishing 2023

Copyright © 2022 by Matthew Mercer

All rights reserved. No part of this publication may be reproduced, stored or transmitted in any form or by any means, electronic, mechanical, photocopying, recording, scanning, or otherwise without written permission from the publisher. It is illegal to copy this book, post it to a website, or distribute it by any other means without permission.

This novel is entirely a work of fiction. The names, characters and incidents portrayed in it are the work of the author's imagination. Any resemblance to actual persons, living or dead, events or localities is entirely coincidental.

Matthew Mercer asserts the moral right to be identified as the author of this work.

Matthew Mercer has no responsibility for the persistence or accuracy of URLs for external or third-party Internet Websites referred to in this publication and does not guarantee that any content on such Websites is, or will remain, accurate or appropriate.

Designations used by companies to distinguish their products are often claimed as trademarks. All brand names and product names used in this book and on its cover are trade names, service marks, trademarks and registered trademarks of their respective owners. The publishers and the book are not associated with any product or vendor mentioned in this book. None of the companies referenced within the book have endorsed the book.

ISBN: 979-8-9868956-4-2

For future projects, consider joining our newsletter at https://aspectsentertainment.com/

You can also follow us on Facebook and Instagram @aspectsentertainment

and Tiktok and Twitter @aspectsent

First edition

Cover art by MiblArt

IT CAME FROM ABOVE

MATTHEW MERCER

For Natasha

"That's what the movies would have you think, but I don't believe it. That just doesn't make sense."

Contents

Preface	VII
Content Warning	VIII
Acknowledgements	IX
Chapter 1	1
Chapter 2	9
Chapter 3	15
Chapter 4	23
Chapter 5	28
Chapter 6	32
Chapter 7	41
Chapter 8	47
Chapter 9	52
Chapter 10	59
Chapter 11	69
Chapter 12	77
Chapter 13	84
Chapter 14	89
Chapter 15	94

Chapter 16	98
Chapter 17	103
Chapter 18	110
Chapter 19	117
Chapter 20	121
Epilogue	125
Also By Matthew Mercer	126
Dedication	129
It Came From Above: A Retelling!	130
Notes From the Author	150

Preface

Writing a story has always been a passion of mine, but I never truly believed that I could. I would spend months at a time trying to come up with the most perfect, thought-provoking, well-written story that I possibly could. It was all a waste of time. I didn't know what I was doing, and hadn't written a single word after all of that time.

One day, I was thinking about slasher films, my favorite kind, and realized that not every story has to be well-written. Alas, "It Came From Above" was born. I glued myself to my laptop and forced myself to write for the next month, until I had a fully developed story, because otherwise, I never would. Now, the characters in this story may not be the most well-written, the plot may not be perfect, and it may not be for everyone. But, I had fun writing it, and I learned what it takes to write a story. If I'm lucky enough, I might've written something that you can enjoy. If not, there's always the next one.

Content Warning

I'll start this with a general content warning. My books may contain graphic descriptions of death, gore, nudity, sexual situations, and many other potentially offensive situations. To keep from spoiling the contents of *this* book, I won't guarantee that everything listed above will be inside, but it might. If any of this offends you, or if you are uncomfortable with your child reading a story containing these contents, this might not be the book for you or them. Otherwise, enjoy the story.

Acknowledgements

With a very loose concept being written by someone with absolutely no experience, there are a few people that I believe are responsible for tying everything together. This book has gone through many stages of suck, and without my editors and proofreaders, it would still be there, so thank you for that.

First of all, thank you to all of my family and friends that gave me any type of support during this whole process.

I would like to give a special thanks to my friends at the coffee shop that gave me free drinks while I worked on this.

Thank you to my beautiful wife-to-be, who dealt with me during my awful writing process, and for giving me the confidence to convince myself that this was something that I was capable of.

Lastly, I want to thank you all for reading. Enjoy.

Chapter 1

Sean

Sean pressed down on his horn. "Come on, we're gonna be late!" He released the horn and gawked in awe as Samantha stepped out of her house. She had long, pitch-black hair that was usually wavy, but she had straightened it for tonight. She wore cherry-red lipstick that contrasted beautifully with her pale skin and a short black dress to match her hair. She waved goodbye to her father and marched down her driveway.

"What were you saying?" she asked as she opened the door of his black Mustang. It wasn't the nicest or newest Mustang out there, but it was his, and it was nice enough to make all of his friends jealous whenever he brought it out.

"I said, you look stunning."

She smiled and held the front of her skirt down as she entered the passenger seat. Sean noticed she had gotten her nails done, a slightly lighter shade of white than her skin.

"Well, I thought, since you were finally brave enough to take me out, I should at least try to make myself look good."

"Amen to that." Sean put the car into gear and sped off, thinking, *She always looked good.*

It was dark by the time they arrived at the drive-in movie theater. Previews for the next big superhero movie release were playing. Luckily, there was no line to enter the lot. As Sean pulled up to the ticket window, he sighed quietly. Trent was working tonight.

Trent was an old friend from high school, but he turned into a real dick when he got denied a football scholarship. He'd burned several bridges over the past year since, and Sean was one of them.

"Damn it," Sean said, rolling down his window, handing him the exact change in thirteen dollars and fifty cents.

"Yooo, my man, Sean! You almost missed the movie." Trent grabbed the cash and peeked into the car.

"Yeah, I know. Can I get the tick—"

"Woah, you brought a girl this time?" Trent interrupted. "No way, Samantha? You two?" Trent laughed as he put it together that the two of them were on a date. "You kiddies have a good time, all right?" He slammed the window shut and waved them into the lot.

"What is *with* that fucking guy?" Samantha said.

"I *really* wish he wasn't the first to find out about us," Sean said.

"You know he asked me out once?"

"No way!"

"Yep. Well, he didn't really ask as much as he demanded. It was right after that homecoming football game last year. I was there with Adalynn, but Trent was positive that I just came to watch *him* play."

"Yeah, that sounds like him."

"Exactly. He found me after the game and insisted I go to homecoming with him," she said.

"I remember that dance. I didn't think you went," Sean said.

"Because I didn't! I tried telling him no, but I think he was drunk. He kept grabbing me with his sweaty football arms." Samantha pretended to gag as she thought about it. "It took Ethan to recognize that I was uncomfortable and get him off me."

"Geez." Sean finished pulling into the perfect spot. Dead center, six rows from the screen. Not too close, not too far. "Well, I'm sorry you had to go through that. I just thought you weren't into dances."

"Of course I am! I just needed somebody *less* gross to ask me."

"Oh, so it's my fault, then?"

"Who says I don't think *you're* gross?" Samantha smiled.

"Well, we're here now, aren't we? That's gotta count for something."

"Not so fast. Let's see how the night goes first." She winked at him and started adjusting her seat. Sean's blush hid beneath the darkness while he searched his pockets.

"Well, that's just great," he said.

"What's wrong?" she asked, still fiddling with the seat mechanism.

"Trent never gave me the tickets. I need them to tell me what FM station the movie is on." Sean started scrolling through stations one at a time before the lights in the car began to flicker. "Woah, what the fuck?" He stopped touching the radio entirely and watched it, puzzled, for about three seconds before his car shut off completely.

"What in the world did you do?" Samantha asked.

"I don't think I did *anything*. I—" His car turned on abruptly, with the radio blasting static at full volume. Sean couldn't get the radio to turn off or even go silent, so they both jumped out of the Mustang. They noticed other moviegoers also getting out of their cars while every vehicle's headlights, as well as the movie projector, flashed on and off repeatedly like strobe lights. It felt like it went on forever, but it took less than twenty seconds for everything to return to normal.

"Are you guys okay?" Samantha asked the family next to them.

"Yeah. Any idea what that was?" The father asked while comforting his two sons.

"None," Sean said. He scanned the area while the family got back in their car. Nothing seemed out of the ordinary. If it weren't for all the confused people standing outside their vehicles, it would appear as if nothing weird ever happened.

"That's so weird." Samantha snuck her fingers between Sean's and pulled him toward the car. "Come on! Let's not let this ruin our night." She scurried back to the passenger seat.

"All right, umm ... How about you mess with the radio and try to find the right station, and I'll buy us some snacks. How does that sound?"

"It sounds like you read my mind." Samantha stuck her tongue out and waved goodbye with her fingers.

Sean started walking toward the concession stand but turned around when he heard a whistle coming from the direction of his parked car. He saw her pale arm stretch outside the window, a pair of black lace panties hanging from her two fingers. With a loud *thud*, Sean walked straight into a plastic trash bin in the middle of the parking lot. From his new seat on the gravel, he saw Samantha giggling through the rear windshield. Embarrassed, he got up and continued walking.

Sean wasn't a fan of the steady decline in drive-in attendees, and tonight there wasn't a particularly busy crowd. There were less than a dozen vehicles in the lot, including his car and the family they had parked next to. Usually, this kind of thing would bum him out, but it wasn't so bad tonight. It was quieter and provided a more intimate vibe for their date. Another plus was the absence of a long line for snacks. Once Sean's eyesight adjusted to the blinding lights inside, he saw that his favorite worker, the drive-in owner, was working tonight. She was a little old woman whom Sean had gotten to know over his years of frequenting the movies.

"Sean! It's so good to see you!" she said.

"You too. I know it's been a while. I've just been busy since I started school again."

"So, what can I get you?"

"Let me start with two orders of popcorn—"

"Two?" she interrupted. "Have you gotten fat since I last saw you?"

"Oh! No, ma'am. I'm on a date tonight, actually."

"A date!" she said, scooping popcorn into the second bucket. "Not my Sean! You've never brought a woman here before!"

"Well, if things go smoothly, I hope to bring her again."

"She better treat you right!" she said. "Hey, Trent! Give Sean two free sodas, all right?"

Sean could feel Trent's presence behind him and dreaded turning around.

"Sean? There he is!" Trent yelled.

"Thank you." Sean grabbed the popcorn from the lovely old lady, who smiled back at him and then turned around, hoping to get the encounter over with. "Wow, they got you all over the place tonight, huh?"

"Everybody's out for vacation since spring break is starting, so I've got to fill the gaps. Did you see all that crazy stuff happen with the lights?" Trent asked.

"That happened here too? That's so weird. All the cars' headlights were flashing."

"Crazy shit, man. What's even crazier is that you're on a date with Samantha, and you're not even getting her some candy."

"Oh, you're right!" While making small talk, Sean had genuinely forgotten. "Can I get some Skittles?"

"Skittles? Really? Didn't think you were that type of guy, but I guess it does make sense."

"Not sure what you're insinuating, but they're for her."

"Hey man, I'm just messing with you. You gotta lighten up sometimes, all right? That's gonna be seventeen eighty-five."

Sean pulled a twenty-dollar bill from his wallet and handed it to Trent, who continued thinking aloud.

"How did you even manage to pull a girl like that? I mean, she's not *much* of a prize, but I never would've thought that *you*, of all people . . ."

Not much of a prize, huh? Sean thought to himself.

"Okay, here's your change." Trent handed it to him, "But hey, before you go! Would you want me to poke a hole in the bottom of one of these popcorn buckets?" Trent held a bucket against his groin.

"No, thank you. As a matter of fact, can I get a new bucket?"

"What did I say? You gotta lighten up!" Trent gave Sean a heavy pat on the shoulder as he grabbed the other popcorn bucket from the counter, causing some to spill.

"All right, dude, thanks." Sean awkwardly held the drinks and popcorn with the Skittles in his pocket and hurried out of the building. *That guy just doesn't get it, does he?* Sean thought.

As he approached the car, he felt nervous butterflies forming deep within his stomach. Samantha had been forward, and Sean had never been on the receiving end of that kind of flirting before. Sure, he had flirted with girls, especially Samantha, but this was the first time for him that *something* might come of it.

He spent the length of the walk overthinking the best thing he could say to match her boldness. When he finally returned to the car, he put the drinks on the roof to open the door and blurted out the only thing he could think of.

"I paid for *your* snacks, so I hope you've got mine ready—" He dropped the popcorn. He thought his eyes were playing tricks on him. She wasn't there. Sitting right where he had left her, Samantha's black dress lay flat against the car seat, and she wasn't in it. Her flip-flops remained on the floor of the car as well. His eyes darted to the backseat, assuming she had stripped down and found her way back there, but his heart sunk even further when he saw it was empty.

Confused, he stepped back from the vehicle and briefly looked around. The movie had finally started to play on the screen behind him, and nearby cars honked at him for distracting them. He dropped to the ground and checked under the car, but no sign of her. He ran to the back of the car and popped open the trunk. Nothing was there but an old English textbook and some beach towels.

Where the fuck is she? Sean thought while the man in the car beside his rolled down his window.

"Hey, dude, can you just get back in your car? We are trying to watch a movie here!" he said, suspenseful orchestral music echoing from his radio.

"Have you seen the girl I was with? She's not here," Sean said.

"She probably went to the bathroom. Or she ditched you. I don't really care!" The man laughed as he rolled up his window.

Sean looked toward the bathroom, and it looked abandoned. *She wouldn't go to the bathroom naked,* Sean told himself. *Where the fuck is she?*

He ran to the passenger side of the car. Right outside the door were the panties that she had teased him with. Now the panic had *really* started to sink in. What were once nervous butterflies in the pit of his stomach were now these uncontrollable, raging hornets.

"What the—?" Sean jumped at the sound of someone walking up from behind him.

"Is there a problem here?" Trent asked, blinding Sean with a flashlight, "Oh, shit, it's you! Dude, what the hell are you doing? You're distracting people from the movie! We've got people coming in to complain, and a bunch of cars were honking and everything. I mean, what the hell?"

"It's Samantha! She's not here!"

"What do you mean?"

"I mean, she's not fucking here! I came back to the car, and she's gone!"

"I'm gonna need you to lower your tone."

"Are you serious? I'm telling you, Samantha is missing!"

"She's probably taking a piss or something. Just get back in your car."

"Pissing without these?" Sean passive-aggressively held out the panties he picked up from the floor.

"It's not like she needs them."

Sean opened the car door and pulled out the dress. "Yeah, I guess she doesn't need any of her other clothes *either*."

Trent's eyes widened as he realized the situation was more serious than he thought. "Oh shit, okay. You stay here, and I'll get the police." Trent sprinted back to the concession stand while Sean paced in circles around his Mustang.

Where the fuck is she? The thought continued to bounce around his head. *Where the fuck is she? It's only our first date. How could I have let her go missing? Where the **fuck** is she?*

As the flashing lights of the cop cars pulled into the parking lot, Sean had one final thought. *I should've never left her alone.*

Samantha's Phone:
How's the date going so far?
Samantha?
Hello?
—Cynthia

Chapter 2

Emma

Ethan stood at the front door with nothing but a towel wrapped around his waist. "Oh, it's you guys." Best friends, Cynthia and Emma, had been pounding on the door for at least three minutes before he answered.

"We were worried about you!" Emma said. The truth is, she was *always* worried about *everyone*. Her friends joked that she was the group's mom because she tried so hard to ensure everyone was always happy. She was an emotional mess, which had her in a constant state of anxiety. At least this time, she had genuine cause for concern.

"Why isn't anyone answering their fucking phones?" Cynthia asked. She and Emma may have been best friends, but they weren't very similar. Cynthia had a more aggressive personality and often rubbed people the wrong way. She barged into the doorway, lightly shoving Ethan out of the way as she made her way to his couch.

"*Sorry!* As you can see, I was in the shower!" he said.

"What's up, bitches?" Adalynn said, making her way down the stairs. She was Ethan's younger sister by a year, making her one of the last high schoolers in the group. Apart from Ethan's stocky, athletic build and Adalynn's slimmer figure, people often mistook them for twins since they looked so similar. They had dirty blonde hair with smiles that were somehow brighter than their hazel eyes, which complemented their tan complexion. In the same fashion as Emma and Cynthia being polar opposites, Ethan and Adalynn genuinely couldn't be any more different.

Everyone who got to know Ethan thought he was the most remarkable person in the world. Borderline perfect. He seemed to have some involvement with *every* crowd through his many hobbies and talents, be it sports, music, art, video games, you name it. He was nice to everyone unless they were making someone else uncomfortable, and his smile could brighten anyone's mood.

While Adalynn shared his smile, people spent more time tolerating her company than enjoying it. She carried herself in a condescending manner as if you ought to feel grateful you were allowed to breathe in her presence. She was the prettiest girl in town, and she knew it.

"Quit being gross and put some clothes on," Adalynn said.

"I wouldn't have needed to answer the door like this if *you* just got off your ass," Ethan retorted.

"My makeup wasn't done—"

"Look, no one cares," Cynthia interrupted. "You guys haven't heard from Samantha, have you?"

The siblings exchanged looks and shook their heads.

"Fuck," Cynthia said, slowly exhaling as she turned on their TV.

"What's going on?" Ethan asked while she changed the channel over to the news station. A live aerial video of the drive-in movie theater was on the screen as multiple cop cars filled the parking lot. A poorly cropped photo of Samantha at a theme park on their senior trip filled the right half of the screen. Beneath it was the headline.

"Local Girl Mysteriously Disappears during Movie Date"

"Oh my god, Samantha!" Ethan said.

"I've been trying to get a hold of her since last night," Cynthia said.

"Wait, it says she was on a date? Who was she on a date with? I think that's the only mystery. He obviously did it," Adalynn said.

"It was Sean," Emma muttered.

"*Sean*? Really?" Ethan said.

"Yeah, we weren't supposed to know, but Samantha was so excited she couldn't help but tell me."

Wow, so he finally did it, huh? I didn't think he had it in him." Ethan mused.

"Who the fuck takes someone out on a Wednesday night?" Adalynn said.

"You guys are missing the point!" Cynthia shouted. "Samantha is *missing*."

"Well, has anyone talked to Sean?" Ethan suggested. "Maybe call him?"

"I wouldn't. Don't wanna be an accessory to murder," Adalynn said.

"Don't even joke about that—" Ethan stopped as a new headline appeared on the screen. "Wait, turn that up." The news anchor seemingly confirmed the room's fear as he spoke.

"This just in. The police have confirmed the identity of the suspect taken into custody last night. Sean Fuhrman, the young lady's date for the evening. At the scene, we have the witness working last night and responsible for calling the police."

"Oh my god," Ethan said as the camera panned over to Trent.

"So, sir, I hear you were not only there last night, but you were actually friends with the victim?" the on-scene anchor asked.

"Yes, ma'am. Friends with both of them, actually. It really hurts to see something like this happen," Trent said earnestly.

"Would you mind sharing the events of what happened last night in your own words?"

"Of course. I was working at the ticket booth when the two of them arrived. I saw her in his passenger seat and everything. Not too long after,

I ran into Sean alone at the concession stand. Right after he left to return to his car, people complained that someone was distracting them from the movie. I went to check on it, and Sean was there holding the clothes she had been wearing, but she was just... *gone*."

"And that's what you told the police?"

"Yes, ma'am."

"So, what do you think really happened last night?"

"Honestly, I don't know. I hope Sean had nothing to do with it, but I can't say for sure. The whole thing is just fishy. I mean, people don't just *disappear*."

"All right, well, that's enough—" The news anchor went silent, and the screen went black. Cynthia had shut off the TV in frustration.

"That guy's a fucking *idiot*," she seethed.

"Well, we don't know what happened," Ethan said. "But it doesn't sound like something Sean would do."

"Of course, it doesn't! He isn't like that!" Emma said. "He's wanted that date for *years*, and you think he would hurt her when it finally happened?"

"Maybe. Maybe it wasn't going well. Who knows?" Adalynn said.

"Bullshit!" Cynthia replied forcefully.

"All right, can we all just calm down? The cops are doing their job searching for her. Soon enough, they'll find her, and she will say what *actually* happened. Until then, speculating won't help anyone," Ethan said.

"That all sounds good, assuming they find her alive," Adalynn said.

"Okay, seriously, you're only making things worse. I'm gonna call Trent and see what's up. You guys wait here." Ethan picked up his phone from the coffee table and walked upstairs.

"So, you guys really don't think Sean had something to do with it, do you?" Adalynn asked.

"Of course not! I mean, you know him. He wouldn't hurt a butterfly. And he's had a thing for Samantha since we were kids," Emma said.

"People do crazy things for love."

"Yeah, but Sean isn't crazy," Cynthia said firmly.

"We don't know that. Psychopaths are often deceptive."

"Okay, enough. Sean didn't do it," Emma said. Adalynn's words started to frustrate her because she couldn't bear the thought of not only her friend getting hurt but also someone she'd known for so long being the cause of it. They sat awkwardly in the living room, waiting for Ethan to come back downstairs.

"So, are you guys going to the fair this weekend?" Adalynn finally asked, breaking the silence.

"Seriously? Our friend is missing, and you're worried about the fair?" Cynthia said.

"I'm just making conversation. Geez." Adalynn rolled her eyes. "Maybe she will be found by then, and we can all go together!"

Cynthia shook her head in disappointment.

"Yeah. That sounds nice," Emma said. They all looked up at Ethan as he walked back down the stairs, this time with clothes on.

"What did he say?" Cynthia asked.

"Not much. But I did convince him that Sean couldn't have had anything to do with it. He's gonna go to the police and tell them the same. Hopefully, that will help get him out of there."

"Hopefully. Sean isn't the jail type. There's no way he could last a full day in there," Cynthia remarked.

"I sure hope you guys are right about this," Adalynn said.

"I just hope we can find Samantha. Nothing else really matters," Ethan replied heavily.

Cynthia got up from her seat on the couch. "Okay, well, we should get out of here. Stay safe and answer your phones, please," she added.

"You too."

Emma's Phone:
*I know you're worried about
Samantha, but we both need
new outfits for the fair.
LMK if you wanna go
shopping!*
—Adalynn

Chapter 3

Cynthia

Emma put her car into drive and peeled out of Ethan's parents' driveway. "God, she's such a bitch!"

"Who?" Cynthia asked.

"Adalynn. First, she accuses Sean of doing some heinous shit, and now she wants me to take her shopping." Emma slammed her hands on her steering wheel. "I can't *stand* her sometimes."

"I know. Me neither. But let's just ignore her. She always has to make things more dramatic than they need to be." Cynthia could feel her body press closer to her seat as Emma pushed harder on the gas. She placed her hand on Emma's thigh and tightly squeezed it. "Hey, I'd at least like to make it home."

Emma let off on the gas and slowly transitioned back down to the speed limit. "Sorry. You know how I get worked up over these things."

If Cynthia had a choice, she would be driving herself home, but between a busy school life and taking care of her little brother while her parents were out of town for work, she had little time to learn to drive. Not to mention even *affording* a vehicle on a college student's budget.

On the other hand, Emma had been smart enough to work through high school and save up enough to get a car of her own. It was a piece of shit Corolla that was even older than they were, but it got her wherever she needed to go. Often, that was her friends' houses.

Cynthia's house was the one farthest from everyone else, but Emma never seemed to mind. Cynthia would at least offer gas money in exchange for rides, but Emma never accepted. Instead, she would joke that Cynthia owed her hundreds of rides in return whenever she managed to acquire a car of her own.

"Are you gonna be okay getting home?" Cynthia asked as she stepped out of Emma's car and onto her driveway.

"Hopefully."

"That's not funny. Don't drive like a crazy person. And you better answer your phone when I call later. I don't want any more friends disappearing."

"Of course. And you too!"

Cynthia waved goodbye while Emma reversed onto the street and faded away in the distance. She walked up the steps to her nice, two-story suburban home. It was a quiet neighborhood where everyone usually kept to themselves, and it had been crime-free for the nineteen years she had lived there. Upon entering her home, she felt a rush of tension and discomfort and was greeted by disconcerting silence. It was the middle of the day, and both her parents' cars were parked outside, but there weren't any signs of life inside. Her father had been a truck driver her entire life, so he was away from home more often than not, and as soon as Cynthia turned eighteen, her mother began joining him on his job. She believed that Cynthia was old enough to care for her little brother, Damien, who was only eight years old. Cynthia didn't agree. She thought Damien should have one of his parents around like she did when she grew up, but her mother was sick of raising kids after almost two decades and wanted to spend more time with the man she fell in love with.

Her parents did try to make it up to them when they came home by spoiling them with all kinds of activities like taking them to baseball games, buying them fast food all week, sometimes fancy restaurants, often showering them with presents, or even throwing parties for all of their friends. Her parents had just returned to town last night, went to bed immediately upon arrival, and were now gone again.

"Hello?" Her voice echoed through the hall as she hung her purse on the coat rack next to the front door. She silently kicked off her Nike high-tops and cautiously walked down the hall toward the kitchen, the floorboards creaking below her feet with every step. She peeked around the corner and saw nobody in the kitchen. However, the refrigerator had been left open. "You'd better not be fucking with me!" she yelled out, grabbing a kitchen knife off the counter. She closed the refrigerator and turned to continue inspecting the home.

THUD

The sound had come from upstairs. Cynthia clenched the knife and headed for the stairs. She thought to call out again but decided that if there was an intruder, she better not expose herself further. She peeked into her parents' room—nobody there—and was startled by the sound of the TV being turned on in her bedroom.

She could feel herself sweating as she tightly gripped the knife and approached her bedroom door. When she began to slowly push the door open, a figure jumped out from behind. Cynthia raised her knife in preparation to defend herself.

"BOO!" the figure shouted.

"Damien! Oh my gosh." Cynthia dropped the knife and hugged her little brother while he laughed hysterically. "Shouldn't you be in school?"

Her parents stepped out of Damien's room next door.

"It's his first day of spring break!" her mother, Laurie, said. Cynthia got her blonde hair and brown eyes from her mom, but her massive height remained a mystery. She stood at least six foot one, while her mother was a measly five foot three on a good day.

"He insisted on starting his vacation by scaring the shit out of you," her father, Thomas, added. Cynthia's facial structure closely resembled her dad's, and she would be the spitting image of him if she had his blue eyes. He was only five foot nine in height, but he had the same brawny, muscular structure as Cynthia, making him look significantly bigger.

Cynthia held her hands over Damien's ears and whispered the words, "I almost stabbed him," to her parents, then kissed him on the forehead.

"I got you good!" Damien yelled with an uncontainable smile on his face.

"Yeah, you did, buddy." Their father lifted Damien up and mussed his hair. "Come on, we're going to get this spring break started off right. We're gonna go grab some pizza."

Cynthia stood up, her heart still beating out of her chest but feeling more relief with every breath she took. Pizza sounded great.

Cynthia leaped out of bed to the sound of violent screaming. Once her blurry vision had cleared, she found she wasn't in her bed at all. She was in her living room, and only a few feet away, Damien slept peacefully on the couch she had just been sleeping on.

She heard the scream again and turned to see the slasher film they had fallen asleep to still playing. She picked up her phone, which told her it was half past midnight, and she had only a single text from her father telling her to put the leftover pizza in the fridge before she went to bed. She looked down at the empty pizza box on the ottoman and giggled at the thought of Damien finishing the rest while she slept.

She grabbed the light blanket that hung over their sofa and threw it over Damien before picking up the TV remote and turning it off. Along with the TV screen, the rest of the house went pitch-black. Cynthia let her eyes adjust to the darkness before sneaking through the house, trying not to wake anyone.

She made it up to her bedroom and got out of the clothes she'd stained with marinara sauce and soda during the horror-movies-and-pizza party with her little brother. She carelessly brushed her teeth through her barely-even-awake level of exhaustion but skipped her usual nighttime shower. Instead, she picked up an oversized T-shirt from the corner of her headboard, threw it over her naked body, and collapsed into bed.

Unfortunately, this was just the beginning of a long night. She tossed and turned, unable to sleep for about two hours. She felt like she was in some state of purgatory, trapped between feeling too tired to function and wide awake. She couldn't stop thinking about Samantha, hoping they had found her by now, but knowing they hadn't because she would've heard something from somebody, anybody.

Trying to get her mind off the situation, she reached for her TV remote under her pillow, where she usually kept it, but it wasn't there. She reached over to her backup spot on the nightstand, trying to keep her eyes closed, and knocked over her digital alarm clock.

"Fuck!" she loudly whispered, noticing the clock's display: 2:57 a.m. Choosing to ignore it, she picked up her remote from the nightstand and pressed the power button, but it didn't work.

What the hell? Batteries must be dead, she thought, throwing off her blanket and jumping out of bed to turn the TV on manually, which didn't work either. That confused her until she remembered the light switch near her door operated the outlet the TV was plugged into. She walked over to flick it on, but it already was. *Must be a power outage,* she thought, yet the digital clock wouldn't have been working if that were the case. She stooped to confirm the TV was plugged in but couldn't see behind her entertainment center in the dark. She stood up, and suddenly her TV screen turned to static. It made her heart skip, but she calmed herself with a deep breath. *That's better than nothing, I guess,* she thought, grabbing the remote once again. Cynthia watched the screen flicker on and off until it hurt her eyes. It continued for about fifteen seconds before it shut off completely.

"What the fuck?" She pressed the power button on the remote repeatedly, each time harder than the last, until she just tossed it onto her bed. *Piece of shit.* Giving up on the TV idea, she thought a glass of water might calm her down, so she headed downstairs. She could hear her father snoring as she descended the stairs, holding her shirt down in case Damien managed to wake up.

There's no way he doesn't wake up, she thought, as the stairs creaked with every step she took. She peeked over the banister but couldn't see anything in the darkness. Assuming she was safe through the silence, she stepped down and tiptoed into the kitchen. Using the dispenser on the fridge door, she went to fill a glass of water and, without much thought, started with the ice. She stopped immediately when the ice maker made its usual *screech*. She stood in silence, waiting to hear any movement from the living room, but instead heard the curtain flapping loosely against the back door.

It can't be, she thought, only confirming her suspicions as the cold breeze grazed across her ankles. *The back door is open? Did I leave it open?*

She yelped as the TV in the living room turned on—playing the same scream that had woken her up earlier—and startled her enough to drop her glass on the floor, which shattered into pieces.

"Damien? Are you awake?" she asked, but there was no response. She took a big step, trying to avoid the broken glass, but pressed her heel directly onto a small shard. "Fuck!" she yelled as she peeled the piece of glass from her foot, staining her fingertips with the small bit of blood that oozed out. "Seriously, if you're just trying to scare me again, this is *not* the time."

She limped through the dining room and into the living room, flicking on the light switch. She noticed that Damien had moved since she had gone upstairs. The blanket she put over him was piled loosely on the floor, and the sliding door to their backyard had been left open. She looked back to the kitchen and saw the bloody trail that followed her from the refrigerator.

"Damien? Where are you? You are in a bunch of trouble!" she said. *Maybe he's sleepwalking again?*

Suddenly the TV screen started to flicker just as her own had before it shut off along with the living room light.

This room too? she thought, holding her hand to her heart as she felt her chest tighten with every breath. She calmed herself down by focusing on each breath individually, counting "one . . . two . . . three . . ." until her nerves felt at ease. *It's too late for this shit,* she thought. The wind violently blew the curtains open as if they were inviting her outside.

"Damien? Are you out here?" She whispered into the night, aware that her parents often slept with their window open, which was located above the back door. "This shit isn't funny! It's time for bed! Both of us!"

She stepped onto the back porch. The feeling of dusty concrete slabs beneath her bare feet shot goosebumps up her arms. A chill went up her spine as the cold breeze blew in from beneath her shirt, causing her to officially regret her chosen sleep attire.

"It's fucking cold out here!" she said, rubbing her arms across her chest. *What the—?* Her attention was drawn to something on the lawn. She ran across the lawn, ignoring the sharp rocks in the mud cutting into her feet, thanks to the adrenaline coursing through her. She made it to the center of the grass, afraid to confirm her fears.

Lying in front of her were the same clothes Damien had been wearing when she'd tucked him in on the couch.

"Damien!" she screamed, causing her parents' light to turn on in their bedroom window. She ran around in the backyard, but he was nowhere to be seen. She fell onto the grass, gripping his clothes and crying. *Why didn't I just bring him up to bed? How could I let this happen?*

Cynthia's Phone:
Hey, Emma hasn't responded.
Would you wanna go shopping in the morning?
—Adalynn

Chapter 4

Emma

Emma finally arrived home, about ready to collapse from exhaustion. Her final week before spring break had been filled with nothing but midterms and essays, and the added anxiety from Samantha and Sean's situation gave her a migraine that threatened to make her head burst. She trudged slowly from the parking lot to her studio apartment's doorstep, dragging her lanyard full of keys along the floor.

"Fuck," she muttered, struggling to fit her key into the hole. She let the door slam against her interior wall after kicking it open and then dropped her purse and keys on the floor next to her coat rack, causing a loud echo to bounce off the bare walls. She held her breath as the noise echoed across the house, worsening her migraine to the point her head pounded even harder, and she dove face-first into her small sofa. She closed her eyes, hoping a brief nap would make the pain go away, but her mind wouldn't stop racing at the thought of Samantha's disappearance.

I swear, Sean better not have had anything to do with this, she thought as she pictured his apartment three doors down from her own. *No!* She slapped her face a few times to snap herself out of it. *Sean would never do something like that.* She shot upright, and her headache came rushing right back. She looked toward her bathroom, spotted the medicine cabinet, and slowly made her way over to it. She scavenged through it, pulled out a bottle of Extra Strength Tylenol, popped it open, fished a couple out, and then entered the kitchen.

She glanced into her empty refrigerator. Typical college life. She opened her cabinet, pulled out a bottle of red wine, and poured herself a glass.

Should I drink this with Tylenol? She paused, dismissing the thought as soon as it came. *I might as well make the* stress **and** *the pain go away.* She popped the pills into her mouth, washed them down with four large gulps of wine, and poured herself another glass. "I'll be back for *you*," she told her wine glass, then ambled to the front door to kick her shoes off.

She headed to the bathroom and started drawing a bath, adjusting the water until it felt hot enough to sting but not scald. She slipped out of her clothes, strolled to the kitchen, picked up the glass of wine, and plopped onto the couch.

"*Much* better." She kicked her feet up to rest on the coffee table and let out a deep sigh. She hoped to find some news about Samantha on TV, but instead, the local news chose to cover a vicious murder that had occurred in a shadier part of town.

"Once again, a poor family of five has been found brutally murdered in their own home. We have no information on a suspect currently, but the police are doing their—" Emma turned off the TV, unable to handle any more negativity. She closed her eyes and thought of Samantha until her eyes started to water. Her breathing grew heavier, as though someone was pressing their hands down on her chest.

Oh shit, the bath! She opened her eyes to find steam throughout her entire apartment, and she jumped off the couch, dashing into the bathroom to turn the water off. *Perfect timing.* The bath had just finished filling up. She pranced back into the living room, grabbing her wine glass, a pumpkin spice scented candle, and a book of matches from atop the coffee table. Her heart skipped a beat when she noticed she had left the curtains open while gallivanting around her apartment in the nude. She peered outside, then pulled them shut.

Welp, someone might've gotten a show, she thought, shrugging her shoulders. *I'm not going to let something else stress me out tonight.*

Back in the bathroom, she lit her candle and set it on the toilet lid, placed her wine glass on the floor near the back of the tub, and dipped her toes in the bath to test the temperature. It had cooled down enough for her to safely submerge herself, allowing the hot water to slowly embrace her inch by inch. She crossed her legs and rested her feet outside the water on the corner of the tub. She closed her eyes and began to lose track of time as she sipped her wine. Her muscles began to relax, and she could feel her built-up tension slowly fading, along with her consciousness.

Emma's eyes snapped open as soon as the bathroom lights flickered until the lights shut off completely. She took a large gulp from her glass.

Thank God for candles. She surveyed the dimly lit bathroom. A glance at the gap between the floor and the bottom of the bathroom door confirmed that the lights had shut off on the other side as well. She froze in place when she heard a muffled voice. Finishing off the glass in one last gulp, she raised herself up and out of the tub as silently as she could. Dripping wet, she left massive puddles on her tile floor as she tiptoed to the door, leaning her ear against it. She couldn't discern where the voices were coming from or what they were saying. She twisted the doorknob, reluctant to open it. Peering into her living room, it surprised her to find the TV still on in her otherwise dark apartment. On the screen, she saw a picture of Samantha next to the accompanying headline.

"Local College Student Disappears from Drive-In Movie Theater"

Didn't I turn that off? She swung open the bathroom door. With no regard for the wet footprints she left on the carpet, she walked through her living room to grab the TV remote and turn up the volume.

"It has been well over twenty-four hours now, and there is still no sign of Ms. Samantha Roberts, who mysteriously disappeared just last night."

BZZZT

Emma jumped at the sound of loud vibration coming from her bathroom. She turned and saw her phone on the bathtub's edge, inching closer to the water with each vibration. She dropped the TV remote and ran to catch her phone before it fell in, but slipped on the pool of water she had left on the floor.

The bathroom spun around her as she lifted her head from the floor. She felt a sharp pain in her temple, right where she slammed into the bathtub's corner. It took her a moment for her vision to realign itself.

BZZZT

Her phone rang once again. Crawling on her knees, she held her hand out just above the water, catching the phone as it slipped off the edge.

"Hello?" she answered.

"Emma—" Static obscured the voice on the other end.

"Cynthia?" She looked down at her phone. "It's like three thirty in the morning! What's wrong?"

"Damien—" Cynthia's voice cut in and out between spurts of static that resembled poorly auto-tuned vocals.

"Did you say, Damien? Is he okay?" Despite how inaudible she sounded, Emma could hear the urgency in Cynthia's voice.

"My back door . . . he . . . clothes . . . there."

"I can't hear you! I'm sorry. Just call in the morning." Emma hung up the phone. She wrapped herself in the towel that hung from a hook and closed the door behind her. When she pulled the plug on the tub drain, her apartment's lights flashed back on.

She looked down at the big, wet mess she had made in the middle of her bathroom. *I'll deal with it in the morning.* She walked into her kitchen to pour herself another glass of wine. The news had already moved on to another story. Plopping herself onto the couch with her drink in hand, she considered her dresser in the corner of the room. *Fuck clothes.* Too exhausted to be bothered, she closed her eyes and passed out in the towel.

Emma's Phone:
Come over as soon as you get up.
Damien's fucking missing!
—Cynthia

Chapter 5

Ethan

Adalynn spun around in front of the mirror while trying on a pair of faded blue jeans, which complemented her green tie-front blouse. "What do you think? Do these make my ass look big?"

"I'm not looking at your ass. Can we just get out of here already? I don't see why you couldn't just wear something from your closet," Ethan said, frustrated that he had to give up his morning to take his little sister shopping.

"Because tonight is going to be special! I can't wear just anything."

"Special?"

"That's what I said!" Adalynn closed the curtain to the dressing room and started looking through her pile of options for what to try next.

"That outfit didn't really scream *special* if that's what you're after."

"See, now you're helping! We'd have been home by now if you were always this helpful." Adalynn slipped off the jeans and picked out a red mini dress she had high hopes for. Ethan rolled his eyes and heard a familiar voice from across the store.

"Yo, Ethan!" It was their big, goofy friend and Ethan's former football teammate, Kyle. He was still a senior in high school and Adalynn's classmate, but his massive build would lead you to believe he was already an all-star NFL player. Ethan's eyes widened as his uncoordinated friend sprinted into the store, bumping into a display and knocking over a pile of neatly folded clothes.

"Don't worry about it," the nearby and clearly irritated employee said, squatting down to clean up the mess.

"What are you doing here?" Kyle asked.

"I've been here all morning with Adaly—"

"Wait," Kyle interrupted, "your fine ass sister is here?" He stood on his tiptoes to scan the store for her.

"Damn, chill!" Ethan said.

"Chill? How am I supposed to ask her to go to the fair if I can't find her?"

"You could try calling. Or texting. But let's be serious. We all know you'll never *actually* ask her out." Ethan spotted Adalynn peeking her head out from behind the dressing room curtain.

"You guys don't know anything. Just watch. I'm gonna ask her *tonight*."

"Oh, Kyle, if we're finally going on our big date this weekend, what do you think of these shoes?" Adalynn ripped open the curtain, wearing a black silk robe over a matching lingerie set and some red high heels.

"What the—?" Ethan looked away in disgust while Kyle's jaw fell to the floor.

"I—I think they look amazing!" Kyle said, staring at her chest rather than the shoes in question.

"Really?" Adalynn blushed. Ethan smacked his friend on the back of his head before closing the curtain on his sister.

"Have some respect." Ethan shook his head at Kyle in disappointment. "And you, put some damn clothes on!" he yelled at the curtain, waiting for the sound of plastic hangers fumbling around on the other side before he felt comfortable walking away.

"Okay, that wasn't my fault." Kyle laughed.

"Sure, but you didn't have to gawk at her like that."

"She asked for my opinion, so I gave it to her." Kyle crossed his arms across his chest.

"Oh yeah? What color were her shoes?"

"What shoes?" Kyle looked over Ethan's shoulder when they heard the curtain opening up. Adalynn stepped out of the fitting room, this time dressed in the clothes that she came in: a black tank top and Daisy Dukes. She held a pile of clothes that hadn't made the cut.

"Our date starts tomorrow at five o'clock. You're picking me up," Adalynn said. She stood on her tiptoes in a failed attempt to match his height and whispered into his ear, "Don't be late."

"Yes, ma'am." Kyle swallowed, watching Adalynn walk away to return the clothes she did not like.

"Wow. You managed to get a date without even asking." Ethan clapped, sarcasm dripping from his voice.

"Yeah, what else did you expect?" Kyle grinned.

"I expected you to actually talk to her. And now, I expect you to go buy her some flowers or something."

"Well, from the looks of things, I don't even need to try with her. She just wants me."

"Right. Good luck with that," Ethan said, watching his sister sift through an aisle of designer coats. *He's really got his work cut out for him,* he thought.

"All right. Well, I've gotta get going. I told Coach Bradley I'd help him get set up for the fair today," Kyle said.

"Sounds good, dude. See you tomorrow, then?"

"Yep, probably at your place when I pick her up."

"Sweet. By the way, she meant it when she said don't be late," Ethan said as a word of caution.

Kyle waved him off and made his way out of the store, bumping into the same display from earlier and knocking over the same pile of clothes the employee had just finished reorganizing.

"Shit, my bad!" he yelled as he jogged out of the store. The employee stomped her foot in frustration and flipped Kyle off on his way out.

Ethan waited outside for his sister to finish up.

"Ready to go?" She stepped out, and Ethan looked up from his phone to see her carrying two full bags.

"Am *I* ready? I've been waiting on you for a whole hour!" Ethan couldn't help but notice the positive aura radiating from his sister's face. She grinned from ear to ear and even *walked* with an excited beat to her step through the mall.

"So," Ethan eventually broke their silence. "Kyle, huh?"

Adalynn stared down at her feet as she kept walking, but Ethan noticed her blushing.

"He's just... He's had a thing for me for so long, so I figured, what's the worst that could happen?"

"Oh, is that right?" Ethan knew his sister better than that. She never volunteered for anything or did something to make anyone outside of her own family happy without at least expecting something in return. He knew going out with Kyle wasn't something she would do unless it involved something *she* wanted.

"Yeah, that's right!" she said. "Now, can we hurry and get out of here? I've gotta get ready for my date!"

"But it's tomorrow," Ethan said, watching his sister prance through the mall parking lot.

Ethan's Phone:
Hey, uh, your sister...
What kind of chocolate
does she like?
—Kyle

Chapter 6

Emma

Emma barely slept that night due to nightmare after nightmare of every horrible scenario that could've happened to Samantha. She dreamt of sex traffickers stripping her clothes off after dragging her from Sean's Mustang. She dreamt of Sean taking advantage of her and disposing of the body in the middle of nowhere. She dreamt of a UFO abducting her and conducting violent experiments before flying off into the night. The dream where she watched Samantha consume hallucinogenic drugs and streak through the drive-in parking lot before being kidnapped by some shady figure hiding in an alleyway woke her up.

Bang bang bang

The violent knock on the door made Emma jump off her couch in a cold sweat. Her heart still raced from the nightmares. They felt so vivid. It seemed like she was actually there. She felt sluggish after being pulled from her deep-sleep state.

Knock knock knock

The second round of knocks indicated somebody more important than a delivery man dropping off a package.

Did they knock that quietly the first time? She finally woke up enough to notice that she stood in her living room completely nude, leaving the towel that had once covered her on the couch. She went to her dresser in the corner and slipped on some light blue panties and a white tank top.

Knock knock knock

"Who is it?" This round of knocks had picked up in volume from the last, heightening her panic and anxiety. *Who the fuck is at my house this early?* Her heart continued to race, not just from the nightmares anymore. She glanced at the clock on her cable box. It read 12:38 p.m. *What? I haven't slept in like this since high school!*

BANG BANG BANG

Emma started to freak out. She didn't want to end up like Samantha, so at the very least, she must warn Cynthia about the psychopath pounding on her door. She picked up her phone to text her and finally saw the text that said Damien was missing. This only worried her more.

Knock knock knock knock

Whoever it was continued to knock incessantly, no longer waiting for her to answer.

"I *said*, who the *fuck* is it?" Emma yelled. Frustrated, she dropped her phone on the cushion and grabbed the baseball bat she had hidden underneath her couch in case of an intruder. She slowly twisted the knob with her sweaty palms and tried to crack open the door without exposing her position.

"Hello—"

"Emma!" The man behind the door shoved the door wide open and invited himself inside. Emma dropped the bat as she fell to the floor, grateful she no longer needed it.

"Oh my God, Sean!"

"Shit, I'm so sorry!" Sean said, helping her up with one hand and covering his eyes with the other. Emma cared less about her exposed state of undress than the miracle of seeing Sean out of jail. She threw herself at him and squeezed him into the tightest bear hug her tiny body could manage.

"Are you okay? I was so worried about you!"

"Yeah, I'm fine," he said, keeping his hands in the air, too afraid to touch her.

She spotted him noticing the disastrous state of her apartment—the towel on the couch, the empty wine glass, the baseball bat.

"I don't remember your place being this messy," he said.

She just giggled.

Then, his face got more serious. "So, have you heard anything?"

"Not much." Emma slipped away from him to pull a bra from the dresser, keeping her back to him while she slipped it on. "Last I heard, you were in jail. And I don't think they've found Samantha yet." She could see his demeanor change at the sound of her name. "I'm sorry."

"No, don't be. They're going to find her. I just can't believe something like this could've ever happened."

"I know, I know. None of us wanted to believe it when we heard." Emma bounced up and down while squeezing herself into a pair of dark skinny jeans. "Listen, I want you to tell me—"

BZZZT

Her phone vibrating on the coffee table interrupted her, and she panicked upon seeing the caller ID.

"Oh shit. Cynthia!"

"Is everything okay?" Sean asked, but Emma shushed him while she answered the phone.

"Cynthia, are you okay?"

"No! You haven't gotten back to me yet," Cynthia said.

"I know. I'm sorry. I slept in, and Sean just showed up."

"Wait, really?"

"Yeah. He's here now. What's going on with Damien?" Emma asked, which led to a long moment of silence.

"He's gone."

Emma froze at her words. She had watched Damien grow up and had even been at their house the day he was born. To hear Cynthia say that he was missing terrified her.

"What do you mean? What happened?" She covered the phone with her hand and whispered, "Damien's missing" to Sean before putting Cynthia on speakerphone.

"I—I don't know. I tucked him in on the couch after watching three scary movies, and then I went upstairs to bed. I came back down in the middle of the night, and he was gone. Our back door was open, so I went outside and . . ." They could hear Cynthia begin to tear up.

"And what?" Emma asked, using a gentle tone to avoid upsetting her.

"I found his pajamas. Just lying there in the grass."

They all fell silent as Emma recognized the look of fear on Sean's face.

"What's wrong?"

"That—that sounds like what happened with Samantha."

"What do you mean?" Cynthia fought to contain her sniffles as she spoke.

"I left to grab us some snacks. When I got back, she was gone. Only her clothes were left."

"Cynthia, we're going to come over," Emma said.

"Okay, that sounds good."

Emma hung up the phone. "So maybe it's the same person?"

Sean shrugged his shoulders. "Yeah, I guess it could be. God, I just hope they're okay."

"Me too. Are you up for a trip to Cynthia's place?"

"Of course."

"Do I finally get to ride in the Mustang?" She held her hands together and fluttered her eyelashes.

"Unfortunately not. The cops kept it for evidence. There's nothing left for them to find, but they insisted on searching for more."

"Hey, don't worry." She picked up her purse from the floor and pulled out her keys.

"We are bound to find something. If whoever is doing this keeps it up, they will slip up somewhere, eventually. They probably already have, and we just need to figure out where."

"You're right," he said as Emma held the front door open for him. They walked in silence until they reached her car. "I just can't shake the feeling that I could've done more. I shouldn't have left her alone," Sean said.

Emma noticed his eyes beginning to water. "It's not your fault! You guys were in a public area. And she's not a child. You didn't have any reason to worry," Emma said to assuage his guilt.

"Well, apparently, I did."

"No, you didn't. Whatever happened, it was out of your control. Who's to say what would've happened if you were there with her? You could both be missing, and we would have nothing."

Sean nodded and got into the passenger seat. "It just sucks. Going through what I went through, just to be accused by the police! And honestly, the worst part of it all is this feeling of guilt. Maybe she would still be around if I was just there with her. Now I don't know where she is or what she's going through!"

Emma started to worry as his composure loosened with each word.

"I don't even know if she's alive! What if she's scared? In pain? What if they're *abusing* her? Not knowing is the scariest part of it all."

"But that's exactly it. We don't know! We have no idea what's going on, so we can't let it affect us. All we need to worry about is finding her. And Damien too."

Sean gave a half-hearted smirk.

"What?" she asked.

"It's just strange. Usually, you're the one freaking out. But here you are, so logical, making sure I'm okay."

"Trust me. I'm freaking out too. I'm just trying to direct my energy into finding a solution. It's hard, but don't think I don't understand what you're going through."

"They left her *clothes* behind, Emma."

"I—"

"I mean, what kind of sick fuck *does* that?" Sean interrupted.

"I really don't know." Emma put the car into drive, and they both rode in silence.

When they arrived, they found caution tape surrounding the house, followed by at least half a dozen police cars along the sidewalk. They could see Cynthia's parents talking with someone who Sean recognized as the lead detective on Samantha's missing person case. Emma noticed that Cynthia's mother's eyes were dry from rubbing at tears all night while her father maintained a stern, motivated face.

Emma parked down the street and walked up to the house. A police officer approached them with his hand up to stop them from entering the property, but Cynthia's mom told him they were allowed to come through. They walked into the house and went straight back to the living room, where Cynthia spoke with who they assumed was another investigator. He was dressed in an all-black suit with sunglasses on despite standing inside a dim-lit room. Cynthia's hair was a mess, tied up in a knotty bun, evidence of a sleepless night. Her cheeks streaked with mascara after hours of tears. She wore striped pajama bottoms beneath an oversized T-shirt. She noticed them walk in but continued to answer the suited man's questions.

"So I know you've been asked this before, but did you notice anything else strange last night?"

"No!" she said. "He was just . . . gone."

"How about before that? Did everything seem normal?"

"What do you mean?" She thought for a second, then cut the man off before he could answer. "Actually, there was something. My electricity was acting strange."

"Can you elaborate?"

"Yeah, my TV was acting like it had a mind of its own. It would turn itself off and on and was flickering super fast."

Emma could feel her heart sink into her stomach.

"Oh shit . . ." Sean said, attracting strange looks from both the suited man and Cynthia. "That's similar to what happened to me!"

"And you are . . . ?" the man asked.

"Sorry, my name is Sean. I was with Samantha Roberts the other night when she . . ."

The man perked up, diverting his interest to him. "So you say this story sounded familiar to yours? How so?"

"The TV flickering. That happened to us at the drive-in. But it wasn't a TV. It was . . . everything. It started with my radio, but then it was everything else. All the cars' headlights, the movie projector, I think Trent even said it happened inside the concession stand."

The man continued to write everything down on a notepad that he pulled from his pocket. Then he took notice of Emma, who had started to freak out. "Did you have something you want to add?" he asked her.

"Me? Oh no!" she said, withholding a portion of the truth. *Weren't my lights flickering last night? Was the killer coming for me next?*

"Okay, well, you guys have clearly been through a lot," he said, closing his notepad. "I think we have enough from you. I've already given Cynthia my card. If you need *anything* or can think of more to add to this story, please call me directly. In the meantime, I suggest you guys find something to take your mind off things. We have the best people on the job, so I wouldn't worry. I hear there's some sort of fair at the high school this weekend. Maybe go to that."

"Thank you," Cynthia said, and the man left them in the living room. She turned to the others, astounded by his nerve. "Did he really just tell us to go to the fair and *not* worry about my missing brother?"

"He might have a point. What are the odds that *we* find them before the police? Or whatever organization that guy works for," Emma said.

"But really? The fair?"

"He means well." Emma tried to reason with her.

"And what about you? I couldn't help but notice you freaking out when we mentioned the lights flickering."

"Yeah, I . . ." Emma rubbed the goosebumps populating the back of her neck, discomforted by the events of the night before. "I went through something similar last night."

Cynthia and Sean both stood up from the couch simultaneously.

"You did?!"

"Yeah, I mean, kind of. My lights in the bathroom flickered, and my entire apartment went pitch-black, minus my TV."

"What the—?" Sean started.

"Yep, that sounds, like, exactly the same," Cynthia interrupted.

"Yeah, except nobody went missing!" Emma said.

"Emma! Why didn't you say something? You could've been *next*!" Sean said.

"I just didn't want to take the investigation off of anybody else. I'm okay. I don't need people searching my house when they should be looking for *them*." Emma pointed at the TV screen with pictures of Samantha and Damien on the news. They were starting to make a bigger deal of the disappearances now that there were two of them, only a day apart. The news lived for stories like this.

"We *all* just need to be more careful from now on," Sean advised.

"Agreed," Cynthia said. "So, what are you guys doing tonight?"

"I guess I haven't thought about it," Sean answered.

"Yeah, same," said Emma.

"Do you want to watch some cheesy horror movies?" Cynthia asked.

"Isn't that, you know . . . kind of insensitive? You know, given the situation?" Sean wondered.

"Only if you think about it that way," Cynthia said. "I figured it could help us think about something else for a while."

Sean looked at Emma and she nodded. "Fuck it, why not?" he concluded.

Emma's Phone:
I just finished shopping,
no thanks to you!
And guess what?
I've got a date!
—Adalynn

Chapter 7

Kyle

Kyle had just finished assisting with setting up the football team's fundraiser dunk tank for the fair. He spent the majority of the day there, along with a couple of other teammates, until he was the last one left. "Do ya need anything else, Coach?"

"Yeah, actually, I need to see if this thing works. Are you any good at throwing a football?" Coach Bradley asked.

Kyle threw him an incredulous look, offended that he would even think to ask.

"Well, go on then! Show me." The coach tossed the ball to Kyle.

"You'd better get up there first!" Kyle pointed at the chair contraption above the glass case they had filled with water.

"Hell no! The fair doesn't start until tomorrow! I'm not getting my ass wet until those kids show up and pay me for it."

Kyle stepped back and threw a bullet pass at the target, missed the mark by a long shot, and sent the football into a popcorn booth behind them.

"Well, at least you proved that I need to set up a net. Some of those kids are bound to be as bad at throwing as you are, so I should make sure they don't hurt anybody." The Coach lobbed a second ball and knocked the target down with ease. The chair released as intended above the water. "That's how it's done!"

"It's a good thing I'm not your quarterback, then."

"Damn right. How about you run to the storage closet next to the locker rooms and bring me over a couple of nets? Soccer, volleyball, it doesn't matter. I'll make it work."

"Thank you, Coach."

"And hey." The coach stopped Kyle from running off. "Don't worry about helping me set them up. I know you still have to prepare for your little date."

"Yes, sir. Thank you." Kyle grinned. "I hope you'll be ready to get soaked tomorrow. You know I'm gonna have to make myself look good in front of her."

"If you're trying to impress a woman, boy, it better not be with that shitty throwing arm."

Kyle laughed off the joke as he jogged through the fairgrounds and toward the locker rooms. He couldn't help but admire how great they filled the place, which otherwise would have been empty during the school year. It looked a little sad without the hundreds of people that would crowd the area over the weekend, but it was still unbelievable the things people had set up in just a couple of days. There were all sorts of carnival games, snack booths, and even a huge Ferris wheel lighting up the center of the fairground.

"Kyle!" He heard a familiar male voice call out to him, and he stopped jogging to look for the source, yet nobody stood out to him. "Over here, dickhead!" The voice came from his left, this time between two game booths. The head of his old teammate, Trent, poked out between two neatly stacked boxes in the aisle.

"What's up, man? What the hell are you doing back here?" Kyle asked.

"Well, I came out here to help the coach set stuff up, but he turned me down. Something about, 'This is for current team members only.' Can you believe that?" Trent sipped from a metal flask.

"Yeah, actually." He watched as Trent twisted the flask closed and wiped his mouth.

"What about you, man? What are you doing out here?"

"Oh, you know, just . . . helping the coach out," Kyle said.

"Oh yeah, right. Sometimes I forget you're a year below me." Trent stood up from his crouched position. Kyle could smell the alcohol on his breath as he spoke. "God, I miss playing football. It's a real shame those colleges didn't want me because of my—" He made air quotes with his fingers. "—poor grades."

Kyle began to feel uncomfortable as Trent crept closer to him.

"I mean, shouldn't my raw talent be *enough*?"

Kyle stepped back, as Trent was now within inches of contact. "Hey, dude, I've gotta get going," he said. "I need to finish up here so I can buy stuff for this date before the stores clo—"

"Date?" Trent interrupted with a raised eyebrow. "With who?"

"You know Adalynn? Ethan's sister?"

Trent finally stepped back, placing a hand on his forehead in disbelief.

"Wow! First, Sean pulls Samantha, and now you get *her*. It's a crazy world we live in."

Unsure of what he meant, Kyle took another step back, now outside the two booths. "Yeah. So, I'll see you later?"

"Definitely, man. The fair," Trent said, sliding his back down the booth wall to a crouched position behind two boxes. Kyle saw him untwisting the cap of his flask as he resumed his jog to the storage closet.

A large metal door greeted him, and he shoved it open; a shrill and loud *screech* echoed in the air, followed by a loud *bang* when it slammed against the inside wall. Kyle entered the room, and the door slammed shut behind him, leaving him in complete darkness. He pulled out his phone to use as a flashlight while he approached the metal shelves along the wall in front of him, quickly scanning them for anything resembling a net, but there was nothing. He was making his way to the entrance when something caught his eye. It was not the net he was looking for.

"Oh my god," he said as he spotted her. In the corner, balled up in the fetal position, with pale white skin and dark black hair, naked from head to toe, was Samantha. Kyle sat her upright against the wall, jostling her for signs of life, but she didn't wake up. He tried lightly slapping her on the cheek but got no response. He then noticed a light rhythm in the movement of her chest. She still breathed. *She's still alive!* Kyle frantically looked around the room. *What if someone finds me with her like this? They'll think I did something to her!* He panicked at the thought.

He slowly opened the door, peeked outside, and saw nobody around. *The coach will come to look for those nets if I don't come back soon. He'll probably think I ditched him for Adalynn.* Kyle had an epiphany; that's right, Adalynn! *Wait, no. I shouldn't stress her out with this. Ethan!* Kyle reached for his phone and dialed, relieved to hear he answered.

"Kyle, what's up?"

"Oh, thank God! Dude, I found Samantha," Kyle said.

"What?"

"I said I fucking found Samantha. I need you to get to the high school and help me."

"What do you mean? Slow down. What exactly do you need help with?"

"Samantha's in this storage closet by the locker rooms, and she's fucking naked. Someone will think I raped her if they find me here, but I can't just leave her like this to go get help. I need you to come."

"Okay, okay, calm down. We'll be there as soon as possible. Just hold on. If I were you, I'd find some sort of weapon in there in case her kidnapper comes back."

He's right, the kidnapper! Kyle thought. "Just be quick, dude. I'm freaking out over here."

"Don't worry. We're on our way." Ethan hung up.

Kyle ran back to the metal shelves along the wall and quickly shuffled through them, ignoring the sound of a metal *clang* behind him. While rummaging through the items, Kyle dropped his phone between the metal wiring on the shelves, blinding him as the flashlight shined directly into his eyes. He closed them, reaching his arm through the gap for his phone, and this time, he heard the *clang* closer as it approached him.

With his arm stuck in the shelf, he looked over toward the noise and spotted the silhouette of a feminine figure holding something. Then, she swung a baseball bat down on his jammed arm, and he screamed, horrified by the *pop* sound that echoed from his shoulder. He pulled his arm from the shelf, slashing the length of his forearm along the metal wiring on the way out, and collapsed onto the floor. He checked his shoulder and gagged at the sight of it hanging loosely from the socket. Kyle crawled backward along the floor, slipping over the trail of blood spilling from his arm.

He thought his eyes were deceiving him as the once-dark silhouette stepped into the light provided by his phone. Slowly approaching, dragging the metal baseball bat in her right hand, was the girl he was trying to help.

"Samantha! What is wrong with you? Did you hit your head? Or were you never really missing?" He screamed in terror as her bare feet stepped through the blood he'd left on the concrete floor. Samantha towered over him, though he could no longer see her face. The light behind her cast a dark shadow over her entire figure.

"Please..." Kyle started to think of Adalynn and how he would finally have a shot with her. He felt regretful about all the time they could've had together if he had only found the courage and asked her earlier. As Samantha raised the bat above Kyle, he thought of how he'd called Ethan to come to this very spot and how he wouldn't have time to warn him of the danger he'd be running into. He let his emotions finally pour from his eyes. "Adalynn, I'm sorry," he said as the bat struck his head.

Kyle's Phone:
Be there in 15 minutes!
Don't go anywhere.
—Adalynn

Chapter 8

Ethan

They were eating at a hole-in-the-wall burger joint when they received Kyle's call, waiting for the bill while the understaffed workers ran around refilling cokes and wiping up spills. As soon as they paid, Ethan packed his sister into the car and sped off. They collected looks from students and staff on campus, helping with fair preparations as they peeled into the parking lot.

"Bring the clothes you just bought," Ethan said, hopping out of the driver's seat.

"What? Why? The fair doesn't start until tomorrow," Adalynn said.

"Kyle said Samantha didn't have any clothes on. Just do it."

"So she gets to wear my stuff before *I* do? I don't think so."

"Now's not the time," Ethan said impatiently, holding the car door open for his little sister. She rolled her eyes and stepped out of the car, shopping bags in hand. They parked at the lot closest to the locker rooms so they didn't have to walk through the entire fairgrounds. Soon they approached the large metal door leading to the storage closet.

Ethan yelled, banging on the door. "Kyle! It's us!" He waited a few seconds before opening the door and letting himself inside. The dim light from the sunset shone in from behind them, illuminating the room with a soft glow. "Kyle?"

No response.

"Hold the door," Ethan said, noticing the light fading as Adalynn began to shut it.

"There she is!" Adalynn yelled, pointing to the corner of the room. True enough, balled up in the fetal position, with pale white skin, dark black hair, and naked from head to toe, sat Samantha. There was no sign of Kyle. Adalynn carefully wedged the door open with one of her shopping bags while she brought the other to Ethan, who ran over to check Samantha for a pulse.

"She's still alive!" he said. "But where the fuck is Kyle?" He lifted Samantha off the floor and placed her back against the wall.

"Quit staring, you perv!" Adalynn yelled at her brother.

"I wasn't."

"Just help me put this on her," Adalynn said, pulling out a pair of gray leggings, a white sweater, and some cheap flip-flops. Ethan didn't recognize any of the pieces from this morning, but he had seen his sister in many outfits, plus it had been a long day. Adalynn lifted Samantha's arms while slipping the sweater over her head. "Help me with the pants!"

"Are you sure?" Ethan asked, refusing to face Samantha.

"Or we could just walk her out of here like this. Yes, I'm sure!"

Ethan kept his eyes shut and awkwardly lifted Samantha off the ground, holding her by her stomach while his sister put on and pulled up the leggings.

"Okay, you can put her down," Adalynn said. Ethan did and opened his eyes. "See? Now she doesn't look so much like a victim."

"But we *will* have to do something about the whole unconscious thing."

"True. Anyways, where the hell is Kyle? Wasn't he supposed to be watching her?"

"Yeah, I don't know. Let me call him." Ethan opened his phone as he stepped outside. He listened to his phone ringing for the entire fifteen seconds before an automated voice messaging system answered. He tried again. And then, once more. Before he could dial a fourth time, Adalynn ran out of the storage closet. "What the—? What's going on?"

"My clothes!" she said.

He looked her up and down but saw nothing wrong with them.

"No, not these! The ones I just bought! They're not in the bag!" Adalynn started to pace back and forth.

"Didn't we just put them on Samantha?"

"The *other* outfit. In the bag I left at the door! It had my dress and heels that I was going to wear on the date tomorrow, and they're gone. Did anybody run by while you were out here?"

"I didn't see anything."

"I didn't *either*."

"You really think someone came by and just stole your clothes?"

"Well, the clothes didn't just get up and walk away themselves!" Tears formed in Adalynn's eyes as she plopped herself on the ground. "Tomorrow was supposed to be special."

"Hey, hey, don't worry. We will figure it out. They probably fell out of the bag on the way over here." He offered his hand to lift her up, but she swatted it away.

"I saw them in there when I put the bag down. It was the last pair of heels they had at that store in my size. Ughhh!" Adalynn released a frustrated scream. Ethan wasn't sure if this was more about the date or the outfit. Either way, he never saw his sister get this bent out of shape over a guy.

"Okay, look. Kyle's had a thing for you for like a decade. He's seen how you look on your *worst* days by now, trust me. He won't care what you wear tomorrow. But even more importantly, we don't even know where he is! And we have an unconscious, kidnapped victim that needs medical attention. Can we just focus on what's important right now? We will figure out your outfit later, I promise."

Adalynn pouted and stood to her feet. "He better not be hiding just to skip out on this date," she said, her tearful voice tremulous.

"Wherever he is, whatever he is doing, I'm sure it's important."

Adalynn nodded her head. They went back to the storage closet and brought Samantha to her feet. They tried putting one arm around each of their shoulders to walk her out, but Adalynn struggled to carry her weight.

"Fuck, we'll never get her out of here like this," Ethan said.

"I never thought this bitch would be *so* heavy. We should just call 911," Adalynn said.

"Kyle? How long does it take to find a damn net?"

Ethan heard a familiar voice entering the building. Coach Bradley.

"Woah, Ethan, what the hell are you doing here?"

"Coach! We need your help. We need to get her to the hospit—" Before he could finish, the coach ran over and picked up Samantha.

"Let's go! Where's your car?" he asked.

"It's just over here in the parking lot," Ethan said.

"You've got a lot of explaining to do with this one."

"Of course," Ethan replied.

Adalynn picked her bags off the ground, and the three of them dashed toward Ethan's car. Along the way, Ethan quickly explained that Kyle had found her in the storage closet, but now they couldn't find him. When they got to the car, Coach Bradley laid her down gently in the backseat.

"I'll go look for Kyle. You guys get her to the hospital. Quick! Do you still have my phone number?" Ethan nodded his head. "Good. Call me when you get there. If you don't, I'm calling the police. We don't know if her kidnapper is here somewhere, so just be careful."

"Yes, sir. And we'll see you tomorrow."

"See you tomorrow."

Ethan and Adalynn jumped in the car and sped away.

Ethan's Phone:
Just wanted to let you know! Sean's back!
—Emma

Chapter 9

Samantha

Samantha awoke to bright lights shining into her eyes, almost blinding her. She felt like she had been hit by a truck while nursing the worst headache of her life. But most of all, she felt confused. She fought through the brightness of the light as she opened her eyes, only to be greeted by a person wearing a recognizable uniform with an unrecognizable face—a nurse from their town's only hospital.

"You're awake!" the nurse said, leaving the room. Samantha heard her voice whispering something outside the doorway. "How are you feeling?" she asked once she returned to Samantha's bedside.

"Okay, I think. My head is killing me," Samantha said. "What's going on?"

"Don't worry. You're safe. Everyone's been looking for you for days!"

"Days? What do you—" Suddenly, she remembered that night. She remembered being in the car, excited to go out with Sean. She remembered watching him trip over the garbage can while she teased him. Lastly, she remembered trying to find the movie audio on the radio before everything went black. "Sean! Is he okay?" A light knock echoed from the door, and the nurse smiled at her.

"I'll let you guys talk for a while," she said, leaving the room as Sean peeked inside.

"I came as soon as I heard they found you," he said.

Samantha looked around to make sure he had a place by her bedside, but the room seemed empty aside from a heart monitor and a table with a bowl of hospital Jell-O.

"Everyone else is here too, but they only let you have one visitor at a time."

"Everyone?" she asked.

"Yeah. Cynthia, Emma, Ethan, and even Adalynn. You had us all worried sick."

"What happened?" she asked, in between coughs. Sean walked over and patted her back—like how one would burp a baby—until the coughing stopped. Samantha noticed that Sean struggled to hold back tears.

"I don't know. I was kind of hoping you knew," he said.

"What do you mean?"

"When I left you that night to get snacks, I came back to the car, and you were gone." A tear ran down his face. "I was so lost. I didn't know what to think. I looked everywhere, and you just *weren't* there. I wasn't sure if you had just left me there or gotten kidnapped or worse."

Samantha just looked back at him with an empty stare. She couldn't believe all this had happened in the blink of an eye.

"How long has it been?" she asked.

"A couple of days." Sean looked away, trying not to let her see him cry, but she knew. "I'm so sorry. Hey, it's not your fault—"

Sean interrupted her, breaking into a bigger stream of tears. "You have *no idea* how happy I am to hear you say that."

"What do you mean?"

"People really think that I hurt you. They even arrested me because of it! They eventually let me go, but people still blame me."

Samantha listened as he poured out his pent-up frustration. "I'm so sorry. That's awful!"

"You shouldn't be sorry. I should. I should have never left you alone that night."

"Stop. It's not your fault. Look at me, I'm alive, and I'm okay! There's no need to beat yourself up."

Sean sniffled and wiped the tears off his face. "You're right," he said after a moment. "I'm just glad you're okay." He squeezed as much of himself as he could onto her bed. "So, how are you feeling? You really don't have any memory from that night?"

"Well, I do remember *some* things." She smiled. "Up until you ran into that trash can."

Sean couldn't help but laugh with her.

"That's so weird . . ." Sean thought out loud. "Whatever happened, they must've done a number on you."

"I guess so. I feel lucky that I still remember our date," she said.

"I think it's unfair," he said, leading Samantha to raise an eyebrow. "I don't want our first date to be a tainted memory. I want a redo!"

"Are you sure?" She shuffled beneath her light hospital blanket, pulling it up and exposing her bare thigh. "We could start up right where we left off." She smiled at the goosebumps that dotted up his arm before the door swung wide open.

"Samantha! Woah—" Adalynn froze. "Am I interrupting something?"

Samantha quickly threw the blanket back over herself.

"Kind of," Sean said.

"Whatever. Samantha! How are you feeling?" Adalynn asked.

"Okay, I think."

"Hey, only one visitor is allowed at a time!" a nurse yelled from the hallway.

"Yeah, yeah." Adalynn rolled her eyes. "Anyways, Samantha. When we found you, you were butt-ass naked, so I let you borrow some clothes and I need them back."

"I was?"

"Yeah. When you vanished, all that was left behind was your clothes," Sean explained.

Adalynn waited impatiently for her clothes with her arms crossed as she rapidly tapped her feet on the ground.

"Oh god. So whoever took me ... Was I—?"

"Nope," the nurse said, barging into the room. "We ran tests, and we saw no signs of any abuse. Physical *or* sexual. You seem to be fine."

"Oh, thank God!" Sean said.

"So, nurse lady," Adalynn said, "where are the clothes Samantha was wearing when we brought her in? I told you guys I needed them back."

"I don't know anything about that. Come with me, and we will figure it out." The nurse pointed a finger gun to her own mouth as she walked out of the room behind Adalynn.

"So what is the news saying about all this?" Samantha asked.

"A whole lot of nothing. Like I said, they believe I did it. They also think some serial kidnapper is out there. Ultimately, though, there aren't any leads," Sean said.

"Serial? Wouldn't there have to be others?"

"Oh my God, yes. I completely forgot to tell you. Cynthia's little brother, Damien, disappeared the same way."

Samantha wasn't sure how to respond. She'd known Damien for most of his life, and she couldn't imagine him missing. "Please tell me you're kidding," she said, her voice soft with concern.

"I really wish I was. Just last night, Cynthia found his clothes in her backyard, and there was no sign of him."

"Oh my God."

"It's gonna be okay. We found *you*, right? And you weren't even injured! We are gonna find Damien the same way."

Samantha felt better in Sean's confidence. She knew he genuinely believed that and had a good point. She had been gone for days, and nothing had happened.

"You're right," she said.

Sean put his hand on her thigh and looked into her eyes. "We're gonna find who did this to you," he said solemnly.

"Maybe it was aliens," Samantha suggested with a serious tone.

Sean looked at her like she was crazy but did not want to say it.

She couldn't hold her straight face for long before bursting into laughter, which quickly turned into a fit of coughing.

Sean cracked a smile. "It's so refreshing to see that you're able to joke right now."

Then, a knock came on the door. Samantha's father stepped inside, and Sean stood up. Samantha expected him to greet her dad with a handshake, but instead, he offered him an apology.

"Sir, I'm so, so sorry. I should've never let any of this happen to her." Her father nodded, and Sean escorted himself out of the room.

"Wasn't that the guy they say did it?" her father asked.

"Well, they're wrong," Samantha said. "Can you drop the protective father act, please? Sean had nothing to do with it."

He walked over and sat in the same spot Sean had just occupied on her bed. "You were supposed to be home by nine," he said, tears in his eyes, while Samantha laughed.

"That's what's upsetting you? Breaking a curfew?" She continued to laugh.

"Of course not! I know you're a big girl now. I just . . ." His eyes traveled away from her. Samantha knew what he was thinking about. Her mother. "I just can't lose you too."

Samantha hadn't thought about how stressed her dad must've been going through all of this. It had been three years, but none of them had ever gotten over it. Her mother lost her life in a terrible car accident. On her way home from buying food for the barbecue they were throwing for Samantha's birthday, she was rear-ended by a drunk driver. Her car veered off the road and into the lone tree on the side of the road. The paramedics declared her dead on impact.

Her father always blamed himself for not going to buy the food himself, and Samantha would blame herself since it was for her party. They would always tell each other they weren't at fault, but that couldn't stop the guilt. And now, her father had to experience losing his only daughter. She couldn't imagine the pain he must have felt or what must've been going through his head the past few days.

"You're not gonna lose me, Dad," she said, placing a hand on the back of his shoulder. "Well, not *again*, at least."

"I know, I just—" The door opened once again, interrupting them and revealing the nurse from before.

"Hey, just so you know, visiting hours are over. I'm really sorry," she said.

"Already? What time is it?" Samantha asked.

"It is just after nine p.m."

Her father stood up from the bed.

"Well, can I just go home now? I feel fine," Samantha said.

"We *highly* recommend you stay at least overnight. We just want to monitor you. Make sure nothing comes up."

"Don't worry. Everything will be fine. We need them to make sure you're okay, especially since we don't know what you've been through. I'll pick you up *first* thing in the morning," her father said.

"Promise?"

"I promise."

She watched as the nurse escorted her father out of the room. He whispered something indistinctly to the nurse as he left.

"Can I get you anything before I leave you alone for the night?" the nurse asked.

"Yeah, actually. Do you know where my phone is?" Samantha asked. She would naturally reach for her pockets, but there weren't any in her hospital gown.

"Unfortunately, I don't. You didn't have much on you when you came in. I'm sorry."

Samantha nodded in disappointment.

"I'll bring you the remote for that," the nurse said, pointing to the small TV mounted in the corner of the room. "And I'll see what kind of snacks I can bring you. But I do suggest that you try to get some rest."

"Thank you so much!" The thought of sleeping hadn't crossed her mind much since she felt like she had been sleeping for days already, but before the nurse returned with any snacks, her mind had already faded away.

Chapter 10

Sean

Sean had a hard time getting excited about being back at his apartment. He was going through a lot. He felt he should be happy about getting some rest, but he couldn't stop thinking about Samantha. She finally returned safe and sound, and he just wanted to be with her.

When they returned to the apartment complex, he walked Emma to her door and continued a few doors down to his own. He fumbled with putting the key in the lock momentarily, then entered his apartment. His roommate Curtis greeted him from his computer desk in the living room corner as he walked in.

"Woah, Sean! Where've you been all day? Kidnap any more women?" he teased, pulling his gaming headset down.

Sean shot him a mean look. The joke was too soon.

"My bad. You know I didn't mean that. I wouldn't have said it if she was still missing."

"How'd you know they found her?" Sean asked.

"Come on. Everyone knows! Our town's too small to keep that shit quiet. It's, like, the only thing on the news right now," Curtis said.

Sean should've known. Even if the news hadn't found out yet, Curtis would have. He styled himself as the kind of guy who would spend his time browsing the deepest conspiracies and internet forums. He often knew things that others didn't, but half the time, they were lucky guesses.

"Still, not a great joke. Cynthia's little brother is missing now, too," Sean said.

"That little kid that's missing? Aw man, I'm sorry. I didn't know. Which one is Cynthia again?"

"The blonde."

"Oh, the tall one? She scares me."

"Everything scares you, Curtis," Sean said, opening the fridge to look for a snack.

"It's a scary world, man. Help yourself to my Hot Pockets. You look like you need one."

Sean looked at the box in disgust, but it had been so long since he had one that they almost seemed appetizing. He pulled one out and threw it in the microwave.

"Thanks."

"So . . ." Curtis leaned forward in his chair. "Did you go see her?"

"Samantha?"

"Yeah, who else?"

"Of course I did."

"Well, spill the details! What did she have to say? Does she know who took her? What happened to her?"

"She has no idea. She says everything went black right around when she disappeared on our date. And the nurses say she doesn't have a single scratch on her."

"You didn't drug her, did you?"

"Really?" Sean tilted his head and glared at him, astounded by his stupidity.

"If not, then there's only one logical explanation."

"Please, enlighten me."

"So, let me just get everything straight. You guys are in the middle of a drive-in parking lot when she seemingly disappears without a single person noticing anything strange going on. You come back to the car, and only her clothes are there. Then, she just appears a few days later with no memory and no injuries?"

"Sounds right."

"Then it was aliens," Curtis said, confident in his claim.

Sean started laughing until he realized that Curtis was serious. "Oh, dude, not you, too," Sean said, pulling his food from the microwave.

"I'm serious. Nothing else makes sense."

"And you think *aliens* do?"

"Well, let's break it down. Were you guys next to any other cars at the drive-in?"

"Yeah, of course."

"And didn't they all yell at you for being a distraction while you were looking for her?"

"Something along those lines, yeah."

"So, don't you think those same people would've noticed if another person came to your car, stripped down a woman, and left with her?"

"They might not have had to strip her. She could've already done that."

"Oh, Sean. You think you're smooth enough to get her naked before the movie even started?"

Sean thought back to when she flashed her panties out the car window. He knew she couldn't have taken everything else off in the short time he grabbed their snacks. Highly unlikely.

"And answer me this," Curtis continued, "when they found her, was she wearing anything?"

"I don't think so." Sean exhaled the hot air that came from the center of his snack.

"Exactly. And if she got out of your car completely naked, someone would've noticed."

"It was dark."

"And she is *super* white. Someone would've seen. Not to mention, she managed to get from the drive-in to a damn high school without anyone noticing her? I mean, don't get me wrong . . . I've seen Samantha. She's a very attractive—"

"Careful," Sean interrupted.

"—very *noticeable* girl," Curtis corrected himself. "If I saw *that* walking around naked . . . I would definitely remember it. And her face is everywhere on the news right now. Plus, they put up posters everywhere. You're telling me that not a single person saw her and thought, 'Oh, that's the naked girl I saw.' It just doesn't add up."

"So that confirms aliens to you?"

"Not entirely, but it certainly helps paint the picture."

"And what does that picture look like?"

"You guys go to the drive-in, you get out of the car just in time, UFO overhead abducts her—leaving her clothes behind because they wouldn't need them—does whatever tests or operations or probing they need to do with her, and disposes of her elsewhere. The high school."

"You're crazy."

"Be that as it may, it all adds up."

"I would've seen a UFO flying above my car."

"If they're capable of space travel and abductions, it's not too much of a stretch to say that they could disguise their ship."

"I just can't believe that there wouldn't be any sign of—"

"There was!" Curtis interrupted. "The news said the drive-in had weird electrical problems that night, right? And the segment about the little boy that disappeared reported similar issues. That had to be some sort of interference the aliens caused when abducting them."

Sean froze. He remembered the headlights flashing and the radio issues. He thought it strange that it affected not only his car but everything else electric in the lot. It didn't make sense then because the cars all ran on their own power, so why would they all have had problems simultaneously? Somehow, Curtis's words were making sense, but Sean refused to believe it. He remembered Emma saying she had similar issues the other night, and he didn't want to indulge the notion that Emma could've been taken too.

"You're crazy."

"That's what everyone says until I'm right. But it's okay." Curtis got up from his chair after closing the game he'd paused. "You are always welcome to come back to me when you realize just how right I am." Curtis walked to the bathroom and turned the shower on. As soon as he closed the door, a knock came from the front door. Sean threw his paper plate away and opened it.

Emma. She wore a matching striped pajama set, no makeup, and her hair tied up in a bun. She also carried a blanket, pillow, and small backpack.

"Emma, what's wrong?" Sean asked.

"I know it's dumb, but I don't feel like sleeping alone tonight. If the lights start doing weird shit again, I'm going to freak out. Can I crash on your couch?"

"You know, usually I sleep on the couch, but I don't wanna be alone tonight either. I'll take the floor." Sean stepped aside so she could walk in. "Wait till I tell you Curtis's theory on what the light flickering is."

"Oh *God*," she said.

Sean always listened to Curtis's theories for entertainment purposes, and he always shared them with Emma. Aside from living practically next door to each other for almost a year now, this was one of the unexpected ways they had bonded, and they'd become really close friends. Cynthia would always be Emma's best friend, and Ethan would be Sean's, but Emma and Sean would become each other's opposite-sex best friend. They enjoyed having someone they could talk to about problems and hearing their different point of view.

Even though they would playfully flirt with each other occasionally, Emma knew that Sean had a thing for Samantha, and Sean knew that Emma would never want to risk ruining their relationship if they took it too far. However, other friends in their group, mostly Adalynn, often theorized that they were dating. Sean worried their friendship would scare away Samantha, so he and Emma made sure to make it a point that they weren't interested in each other whenever possible.

"Thank God I brought a bottle." Emma turned around, showing off the top of a wine bottle poking out of her backpack. "I don't think I can deal with his nonsense on an empty stomach, though. I'm gonna order a pizza. Tell me what he thinks when it gets here."

"Sounds good to me. Extra cheese?"

They sat on Sean's living room floor with the wine bottle and pizza between them.

"So, get this . . ." Sean said, trying not to laugh. "He thinks the lights flickering were aliens disrupting the electricity during their abductions." They both burst out laughing.

"My lights flickered when I was in the bath!" Emma said. "Why didn't they take me?"

"Well, they apparently like to take people's clothes off, and you had already done it for them! Maybe you ruined the fun?" Sean continued to laugh while he sipped from his second glass of wine. "Or they just saw what you looked like naked and ran the other way?"

Emma picked off an olive from her slice of pizza and threw it at him. "Screw you!" she yelled, pouring herself another glass and emptying the bottle. Sean had already lost count of how many drinks she'd had. They heard the shower turn off, and they ate in silence for a couple of seconds.

"How long was he in there?"

"Since right before you showed up."

"So it took him as much time to shower as it did for us to get pizza delivered and kill a bottle of wine?"

"He always takes forever."

The door to the bathroom swung open, and steam filled the apartment. Curtis stepped out with a towel tied loosely around his waist.

"I was starting to think you got abducted!" Sean said, causing Emma to squirt wine from her nose.

"Emma? What are you doing here?" Curtis asked, ignoring Sean's joke.

"Stressful week. People are getting kidnapped. I'd rather not be alone," she said. "If I'm gonna get abducted, I want witnesses."

"Smart girl," he said, grabbing a slice of pizza from the counter. "I'll be in my room. You kiddies have fun." They waited for him to enter the one bedroom in the apartment and close the door before they both broke out into an obnoxious roar of laughter.

"This is great," Emma said. "Much better than stressing in my room about Damien."

"Much better than stressing about Samantha disappearing from the hospital." Sean took another sip from his glass.

"You're drinking more than usual." Emma narrowed her eyes, curious.

"If there was ever a time, it's now. Curtis almost had me believing in aliens! I figured alcohol would stop me from overthinking anymore." He gulped down the rest of his glass.

"Looks like we need more," Emma said. "Wait here. I'll be right back."

"No, I'll go with you," Sean offered, thinking about the last time he had left a girl alone. He rose to his feet and stumbled a little, dizzy from the blood rushing to his head.

"It's just down the hall. I'll be okay," Emma said, catching Sean as he stumbled back. She walked him to the couch and sat him down.

"The concession stand wasn't far from my car, either."

"You have nothing to worry about. Like I said, I'll be okay. And you're too fucked up to walk anyway. I'll be more likely to get abducted if I have to help you get around."

Sean didn't spend much time thinking about it. Emma was smart, and he didn't have the energy to argue with her.

"Just . . . be quick," he said.

"You know you're cute when you're protective. Samantha's going to be really lucky when you guys start dating again," Emma said as she stepped out of the apartment.

I'm cute? Sean thought before he drunkenly passed out on the couch.

He woke screaming and covered in alcoholic sweat when the lights started flickering.

Emma! His mind slowly started to remember where he was, his heart pounding. He heard a soft giggle from the front door and looked over to see Emma with her hand over the light switch.

"Bad joke?" she asked.

"The worst," Sean replied.

"Looks like you might be too tired for any more partying," Emma said, raising her eyebrows as though she were hopeful Sean would still be down. She flashed him the bottle that she brought back from her apartment.

"I'm still up for it if you are," he said, trying to stand up but falling immediately back down on the couch.

"Let me help you." She giggled, grabbed his hand, and tried lifting him, but he still couldn't balance, and she couldn't support his full weight. They both fell onto the couch, causing it to flip onto its back with a loud *crash*.

Curtis came running out of his room.

"Are you guys okay?" He stopped when he saw them. "Wow, Sean. First, you tell me you're a virgin, and now you're bagging two in one week. Good for you." He went back into his room.

Sean realized the awkward position he was in. He lay flat on his back with Emma on top of him, her brunette hair flowing down to the floor from above his face. Their faces were so close, and the way Emma blushed while looking at him made him believe a kiss was coming.

Is this gonna be my first time? This shouldn't be happening, but he felt too drunk to handle the situation properly. *I don't want things to get weird between us,* he thought. *She knows that I want Samantha. But this just feels . . . right?* He tried judging Emma's expression, but he could not read her thoughts. Maybe she was struggling with the same internal discussion as he was. *Wouldn't this be her first too? It's not like anyone would have to know . . .* He stopped himself from going any further. *This must be the wine.* Before he could gather the words, Emma finally broke the silence.

"Oh my gosh, you should see your face! You're so nervous." She laughed. Sean wanted to laugh, too, but he still couldn't tell where her intentions were. "Don't worry," she said, "I want my first to be memorable in a *good* way. Not the kind that ruins a good thing."

Sean couldn't tell whether she was talking about their own friendship or his potential relationship with Samantha. Either way, he felt relieved.

"Now, let's get you some water," she said, climbing off Sean and then walking to the kitchen sink. "You're super drunk."

Sean's Phone:

Are you guys going to the fair

tomorrow?
I know we just found Samantha, but it might be good for her to get her mind off things. Maybe make her feel like a normal girl and not some sorry victim?
—Ethan

Chapter 11

Adalynn

"Please, please, please!" Adalynn prayed as she turned her phone back on. She hadn't been able to sleep the night before because she would jump at every notification bell, hoping it was something that came from Kyle. She forced herself to turn her phone off, insisting that she would have a text from him by the time she woke up, but as she sat on the edge of her bed waiting for her notifications to load, that text never arrived. "Ughhh, I fucking *hate* this!" she yelled, throwing her phone onto her mattress.

The anticipation had woken her up earlier than she expected, and she felt like she needed a shower, but she worried that if she got ready for her date too soon, her hair and makeup would be ruined by the time Kyle came around. *Just real quick*, she thought while she turned the water on. While splashing water on her face, she remembered her clothes were still at the hospital. The nurse had told her Samantha didn't have any clothes for when she checked out, so they hadn't let Adalynn retrieve them. Her mind wouldn't stop thinking about Kyle, so she needed to find something else to do, and that could be it. Harass Samantha for her clothes.

She put on an outfit that was not exactly "date ready" but looked nice enough for her to be seen outside of the house. She brushed her hair but didn't put on any makeup—not that she needed any, to begin with—and ran downstairs to find Ethan awake and enjoying a bowl of cereal.

"Good morning. Have you heard from—"

"Come on, we gotta go," she interrupted him, pulling her purse down from the front door hanger.

"Where are we going?" he asked.

"I didn't tell you? I promised Samantha we would give her a ride home today."

Ethan took one last bite and tossed his bowl in the sink. He ran upstairs to grab his keys and followed his sister out the door.

"Why would she get a ride from *you*?" Ethan asked as they pulled out of the driveway.

"Sean never got his car back from the cops," Adalynn said, lying through her teeth. At least her information sounded right. She'd overheard Sean tell Ethan about his car at the hospital the day before, so she knew Ethan wouldn't question her logic.

"You don't have a car *either*!" he said.

"I'm in one now, aren't I?"

Ethan rolled his eyes. "You could've asked. Or at least told me sooner."

"And you should just be happy to help." Adalynn felt annoyed with all of his questions, but she knew they weren't the root of her problem. Just like the night before, she jumped at every vibration from her phone, but none were from the person she wanted to hear from.

"So, you still haven't heard from him?"

Adalynn felt like crying as she stared out the window, watching all the buildings passing by. She tried to respond, but she couldn't summon the words. Even though all she wanted to say was, "Not yet," she kept getting all choked up. She could feel the pity coming from Ethan, and she hated it. She hadn't been on the receiving end of that feeling in such a long time.

"I'm sure he's fine. He's probably planning some big surprise for you," he reassured her.

I doubt it, she thought. *He's probably just running away from me. Maybe I came on too strong? Maybe he never really liked me.*

"And if he doesn't show up, he doesn't deserve you. He's had years to prepare for this. To throw it all away now would just be ridiculous. You deserve better than that, and I'm sure he has a good reason for wherever he is right now. For all we know, he could've just lost his phone!"

"You're right." Adalynn sat up straight, wiped the tears from her face, and thanked herself for not wearing makeup this morning.

"I just hope he's okay. It *is* weird that he would disappear when we were supposed to be helping him."

"He couldn't have been taken by the same kidnapper. We didn't find his clothes at the scene, like with Samantha and Damien," Adalynn said.

Her statement made Ethan feel better, and she couldn't stay upset when she saw him in a good mood. When they got to the hospital, they went straight to Samantha's room. They were still only allowed to visit one guest at a time, and Adalynn volunteered to go first.

Samantha looked surprised to see her when she walked in, almost certainly expecting someone else. But she seemed happy that someone was there at all.

"You ready to get out of here?" Adalynn asked. She took notice of her clothes, neatly folded on the counter next to the sink in the room.

"You have no idea. I've been bored out of my mind!" Samantha said.

"All right, pack your things, and let's go."

"Wait, my dad said he was gonna pick me up."

"Then let's get you home before he leaves! Come on. We don't have time to waste."

Samantha didn't object. She got out of bed and tightly held the back of her gown as she walked over to grab the clothes. "This is probably the real reason you came, right?"

"Exactly," Adalynn said, not even bothering to lie. "Now, don't stretch them out! Just put 'em on, and you can give them back to me at your place."

"Thank you."

Adalynn felt anxious watching how tight the leggings fit Samantha while she pulled them up beneath her hospital gown. Before she got them past her knees, Samantha noticed her fretful gaze.

"You know, they would fit me better if you weren't so damn skinny." Samantha gave one big pull, and they were on. She started to remove her gown so she could put her top on. "Do you mind?"

"Right. Just meet me outside." Adalynn rolled her eyes and left the room. She caught the nurse walking past. "It's okay if we check Samantha out of here, right?"

"Oh, I'm not sure about that. I believe the police are on their way to discuss her disappearance," the nurse said.

"She *just* came back! And she is super stressed out. Don't you think it's a little early to bombard her with questions? When they show up, just tell them she went home and to question her later!"

"Well, I suppose she can check out whenever she wants to. It's not like we're holding her hostage. Just make sure she lets them know at the nurses station when she leaves."

Adalynn nodded, and the nurse kept walking. As Samantha stepped out of her room, Ethan stood up straight from the wall he had been leaning on.

"Samantha!" he yelled as he ran over to hug her. "It's so good to finally see you."

"It's good to see you too. I'm sorry Adalynn dragged you all the way out here."

"Don't be sorry. I wanted to help! Though I have to admit, I was shocked when Adalynn said she promised to pick you up."

"Is that what she said happened? You know she just wanted her clothes back."

Ethan looked at his sister in disappointment. "Really?"

"I mean, of course, I wanted to see her too! But I just bought those clothes."

"I can't say I'm surprised," Ethan said, rolling his eyes. "Well, let's get you out of here."

They made their way through the hospital to the parking lot. Ethan held the door open for Samantha while she hopped in behind Adalynn on the passenger side. Adalynn pulled out her phone to see if she had any missed calls from Kyle. She didn't.

"Oh, Adalynn, can I use your phone real quick? I should call my dad and let him know you guys are bringing me home."

"Yeah, here." Adalynn tossed the phone to her. "The password is 1015."

"Your birthday?" Ethan asked, bringing out a light giggle from Samantha.

"I'm gonna have to change it now, but yeah."

"Wow, and your home screen is a picture of yourself! You really are the narcissist we all thought you were," Samantha joked. The selfie had been taken at the mall only minutes after she and Kyle had agreed on their date. It was a special moment, and looking at that picture made her happy while she stressed over where Kyle could be. Samantha didn't know this, so Adalynn couldn't fault her for making the joke.

"Do I not look good in that picture?"

Samantha called her dad and quickly told him she was on the way home. "I feel so bad. He sounded exhausted when he answered. I can't imagine he's gotten much sleep over the past few nights," she said.

"Don't feel bad. Of course, he's exhausted. Until we know what happened, you will, unfortunately, cause him a lot of stress. He's your dad," Ethan said, the voice of reason. "You did nothing wrong, and the only person at fault is the guy that did this to you," Ethan continued. He looked back and smiled at her.

"Thanks, Ethan," Samantha said.

"So, I know it's probably not the best timing, with you just coming home and all . . . but I think getting your mind off things might be a good idea. What do you think about coming to the fair tonight?" Ethan asked.

"Oh no way, that's tonight? My whole calendar is all messed up right now from, you know, disappearing. I think it sounds fun. Who's going?"

"Don't you mean, is *Sean* going?" Adalynn said, smirking.

"Okay, fine. Do you think Sean is going?"

"I don't see why not. Especially if you go. I'll be there, and I'm trying to get everyone else to go too. I doubt Cynthia will come since Damien's missing, but Adalynn is going to be there on a date tonight," said Ethan.

"No way! Adalynn on a date? I never thought she'd find a guy she considered worthy," she said.

"It was supposed to be Kyle, but that prick won't answer his phone," Adalynn responded, sulking.

"Really? He'd be crazy to ditch you after all these years. When's the last you heard from him?"

"He was the one that found you. He called Ethan and told us to meet him and get you some help, but when we got there, he was gone. I assumed he had run off to buy me flowers, but it's been almost a full day. I'm honestly worried at this point."

"You don't think—" Samantha bit her tongue.

"Think what?" Adalynn asked.

"You don't think he might've had something to do with my disappearance, do you?"

"No way," Ethan said. "Kyle would never hurt a fly. I can promise you that. And I know he was with Coach Bradley that whole day."

"Okay. Well, in that case, I just hope he's okay."

"He is. Trust me. Kyle's a tough guy. It's far more likely that he found whoever did this to you and has been giving them hell for eighteen hours straight." Adalynn sunk into her seat. None of them knew what could've happened to him, and the more they talked about it, the worse her anxiety grew. She sat in silence, listening to Ethan and Samantha talk over everything that had happened from when she went missing until they arrived at her house. Samantha ran inside and took a few minutes to greet her dad and get dressed.

While they waited, her father came outside and thanked them for bringing her back to him. He knew they were the ones that got her to safety, and he said he owed them the world. He invited them to come inside and have a drink, but they insisted they had to get going—it was too early in the morning to be drinking. Samantha came back outside with Adalynn's clothes and gave them back.

"Thank you both again, really. I don't know where I would be right now if it weren't for the two of you," she said. "We'll have to wait and see if my dad will let me out of the house ever again. If so, I'll see you at the fair. Ethan, I don't have a phone, so I'm counting on you to get Sean to go."

"Sweet. We'll see you there!" he said.

Adalynn smiled at her as they drove away, feeling crippled beneath the weight of her anxiety. *Should I even get ready for this fair? Is there even gonna be a date?*

Adalynn's Phone:
Ethan told me you haven't heard from your date.
Screw that, let's have our own fun!

—Emma

Chapter 12

Emma

Emma's head pounded in pain as soon as she woke up. She would have remained asleep if she had a choice, but if she didn't get up now, she would vomit all over Sean's carpet. Instead, she found herself kneeling in front of a toilet bowl, trying her best to keep her hair out of the way as she finished puking up her disgusting pizza and wine mixture from the night before.

"*This* is why I don't drink," Sean said, rubbing his eyes as he entered the bathroom. "And it always gives me a major fucking headache."

"It could be worse," Emma said, her voice echoing inside the toilet bowl. She flushed it in an attempt to mask the smell.

"Yeah, I could look like you right now." He pulled her hair around the back of her neck and held onto it while she barfed. "Geez, I can't believe you could fit all that in your stomach."

Emma wanted to retort, but she struggled to even breathe. Her throat swelled, and the acidic pizza taste left a weird feeling in her mouth that didn't help.

"Listen." Sean pulled a large bottle of mouthwash from the cabinet behind his bathroom mirror and set it on the counter. "About last night—"

Emma stopped him by holding one hand out as she threw up one final time. "Stop," she said.

"I really think we should talk about it," he pressed.

"There's nothing to talk about. We were both drunk, and nothing happened. There's no point in turning it into something it's not."

"So that's it, then? We were just drunk? There are no underlying feelings that I should be worried about?"

Emma thought about it. If there were ever a time to tell Sean she *did* have thoughts about him, it would've been now. But she worried that their relationship would change. He would choose Samantha over her, especially after what they'd gone through, and she's too close a friend to Samantha to ruin something good for her. Emma might have had a moment of weakness the night before, perhaps ready to risk it all, but she hadn't. As far as she was concerned, that's what mattered.

"None," she said, grabbing the bottle from the counter without pulling her head too far from the toilet. She gargled the mouthwash for about thirty seconds and spat it into the toilet. "I was drunk and horny. I'm assuming you felt the same way. If you'd played your cards right, maybe you could've gotten lucky, and we'd never talk about it again. But now that I'm awake and sober, mostly, nothing will happen, and we *still* will never talk about it again."

Sean looked dumbfounded as she finally stood up, flushing the toilet again.

"Now, I'm going back to my apartment to brush my teeth and get some more wine to cure this hangover. I'll be right back."

Before she left the apartment, Sean stopped her. "Emma, wait."

She felt nervous, imagining that he might have an objection to her decision to pretend like nothing had happened, but her hope was short-lived. She turned and saw Sean reading something on his phone.

"I just got a text from Ethan. He says they just dropped Samantha off at her dad's house."

"That's great!" she said. A part of her was upset that he had nothing else to say, but she stuffed it down, knowing that this was how things were meant to be to keep everyone happy. She was no stranger to sacrificing her own feelings for those of her friends, but these strange new feelings that she had for Sean came out of nowhere. She'd always had a harmless crush on him, but something about it just felt different today. As if the night they spent together multiplied her infatuation with him tenfold, and she started to regret that.

"He also says Samantha wants us to all go to the fair tonight. That sounds fun, right?"

"That *does* sound fun, but I don't know," she said, thinking that she really didn't want to spend the day watching Sean and Samantha cupcake around the fairgrounds. "Something about it just doesn't feel right while Damien is still missing. I should really spend time with Cynthia today."

"Call her! You heard the cop at her place. It would be best if we all had a distraction, *especially* her. See if she wants to come. I think it would be a lot of fun for all of us. And Samantha definitely needs this with all of the shit she's going through."

Emma nodded and walked out of his apartment. Resentment toward Samantha started to grow, and she didn't like it. Emma knew Samantha had done nothing wrong, but she couldn't shake the unfairness surrounding the situation. Emma would never admit it to anyone, but when Samantha had disappeared, she had thought multiple times about a future with Sean being an actual possibility one day. She felt instantly bad for those thoughts, so she repressed them as best she could. She never would've wanted anything bad to happen to Samantha, but now that she had returned, Emma couldn't help but think of what could've been. Whether or not alcohol had a hand in it, she'd felt closer than she ever had to that future last night, and now that she had returned to repression mode, all she felt was anger. Emma quickly brushed her teeth and called Cynthia, who answered immediately.

"Hello? Cynthia?"

"Yeah, what's up?"

"So, I know you're probably not up for it, but Samantha is finally home today. She is wondering if we would all want to go to the fair with her?" Emma hoped that with the proper wording, she could convince Cynthia not to go so she wouldn't have to either.

"Yeah, that sounds great," Cynthia said. "I haven't seen her yet. I think seeing her alive and unharmed might make me feel a bit better about Damien. And maybe I can ask her some questions about what happened that night."

Emma mouthed "Fuck" in disappointment and leaned her head on the refrigerator door, regretting even making the phone call. She jettisoned the hair of the dog cure since she would be driving everyone.

"Emma, you still there?"

"Yeah, I'm here. Did you want me to come pick you up? What time will you be ready?"

"Give me an hour."

"See you then."

Emma texted Sean that Cynthia wanted to go, that she was going to quickly shower and get ready, so he should just walk into her apartment when he was good to go, and she would drive everyone to the fair. Without waiting for a response, she unlocked her front door, undressed, and jumped into the shower. She spent extra time washing her face; she had already cleaned off all the vomit, but she wanted to be sure. When she remembered the lights flickering the last time she had been here, she tried her best to hurry through the process. When finished, she wrapped herself in a towel in case Sean had walked in, which he hadn't, and threw on a green sundress from her closet.

Sean finally walked in as she finished putting on her makeup. She smacked her lips together to smooth out the light layer of lipstick she'd applied.

"Ready to go?" she asked.

"Ready."

"Do we know if Samantha has a way to get to the fair?" Emma asked. Her grip tightened on the steering wheel. The only feeling worse than her resentment toward Samantha was Emma's hatred of herself for feeling that way.

"I asked Ethan, and he said he wasn't sure. He was already on his way, taking Adalynn there. Kyle hasn't been seen since yesterday, so they want to look for him around the school. Would you mind stopping by her house after we grab Cynthia?"

"Will do," she said with as much enthusiasm as she could muster. She'd figured she would end up having to give her a ride—she practically offered just by asking the question— and that the two of them would likely sit in the back seat together while Cynthia kept her company. Maybe she should focus on cheering up her friend instead of brooding over something so stupid.

At three o'clock, they reached Cynthia's house. The day escaped Emma quicker than she realized. Sean seemed to be recovering better, but her headache grew worse with each passing hour. At this point, could it be the alcohol or her stress causing it?

Cynthia's place no longer looked like a crime scene, but an air of depression surrounded it. She looked dressed and ready to go, or at least, as dressed up as they could expect her to be, given the circumstance. She wore tight blue jeans, black Vans, and a T-shirt with her favorite punk band's logo on it.

"Well, you guys look nice," she said, her tired voice sounding hollow. Sean wore a nice red flannel shirt and a vibrant cologne. He obviously had taken tonight seriously, as though it were an extension of his first date with Samantha. Emma—in the sundress she had worn purely for comfort—did not seem to be trying as hard.

"Should I put on something nicer?" Cynthia asked.

"There's no need. It's just the high school's yearly fair. Nothing important," Emma said.

"All right, then, let's get going."

"How are your parents?" Sean asked. "Should we come in and say hi?"

"They left," Cynthia said. "This morning, I woke up, and they were gone."

"Seriously?" Emma said.

"Yeah."

Emma could sense Cynthia's anger toward them but didn't want to keep forcing her to talk about it.

"I knew they would have trouble handling the situation, but geez," Sean said.

"They have trouble with most situations. But it's fine. We'll find Damien whether they're around or not. Now let's go."

Sean held the passenger door open for Cynthia, but she insisted on lying in the back seat. So far, Emma's plans weren't going very well. As expected, Cynthia's presence brought the mood down, so the car remained silent on the way to Samantha's.

Sean thought it would be best if Emma went to the door since Samantha's father probably wouldn't want to see him right now. He came to the door, looking exhausted. She could even smell alcohol on his breath.

"Emma! It's good to see you again. What's up?"

"It's good to see you too. Is Samantha home? We were hoping to take her to the fair."

Her father squinted and scratched his chin.

"I thought she was with you guys, to be honest. She left earlier and said she was going to the fair."

"Oh really? Maybe Ethan ended up picking her up after all."

"Hold on," he said, leaning back behind the front door. "Is my truck outside?"

"Would it be in the driveway? It was empty when we got here."

"That girl . . ." He shook his head. "She took my keys. She must've gone on her own."

"Really? And you said that she went to the fair?"

"I sure hope so. At least, that's what she told me. Do me a favor, will you?"

"Sure."

"Please just find her. I swear she's gonna be the death of me. Make sure she's safe. And stay with her all night. I need her safe. I can't have her disappear again."

Emma noticed that he looked ready to break down in tears. She had hoped to ditch Sean and Samantha early in the night but could not bring herself to tell the man no. He practically begged her to promise him.

"I promise."

Emma ran back to the car.

"What happened?" Sean asked.

"Samantha already went to the fair. She took her dad's truck."

"We really need to get her phone back," Cynthia said.

"Let's worry about that tomorrow," Sean said. "Let's go meet up with her."

Emma's Phone:

Just got to the fair
with Adalynn.
Let me know when
you guys show up!
—Ethan

Chapter 13

Trent

The fair had finally begun, but the party had started early for Trent. He had spent the last hour leading up to the event drinking alone, exclusively inebriated, before any of his friends arrived. Fair attendees scowled at him as he walked by, reeking of alcohol.

I should probably clean myself up. He stumbled over to the men's locker room and flipped up the light switch, causing a single light above Coach Bradley's office door to flicker. Trent set his duffel bag on a bench between the showers and a row of lockers. He started removing his clothes, spilling some of the forty-ounce he refused to put down. After nearly falling twice, Trent dropped his clothes onto the floor and entered the shower. *It's been a while since I've been here.* He turned the shower onto maximum heat. Once he realized his skin was burning, he hopped awkwardly to the corner of the shower and passed his open hand through the scalding stream to turn it down. It burned him so badly that he couldn't reach the shower handle. He yanked his hand away and dropped the glass bottle in his other hand to grip his wrist, now writhing in pain. "Fuck!" He yelled at the sound of glass shattering on the shower floor. He shook his hand to endure the pain while trying to slide the glass shards down the shower's drain hole with his foot, though he couldn't see how big of a mess there was through his alcohol-distorted vision.

Assuming he'd finished, he reached around the water to grab the handle and turn the heat down to a more tolerable level.

Trent wept beneath the shower stream as he washed his face. This would likely be the last time he would be welcomed in this locker room, where he had spent most of the best years of his life. It'd been almost a year since he had left high school, and more and more people were going to consider him weird for hanging around the high school as an adult. But to Trent, this had been the place he loved most. He had been a superstar athlete, joining the varsity football team as a sophomore, breaking all his high school's records as a pass-rusher on the defensive end, and working the offense as a running back. Teammates looked up to him, students admired him, girls threw themselves at him, and his coach regarded him with pride.

All of that changed during his senior year. He'd spent too much time partying, drinking, and working out to focus on his grades. Why would he need to know anything about history, math, or how to write essays if he pursued pro football? He couldn't believe that a five-star recruit like him would not only be deemed ineligible for scholarships but also denied admission to colleges because of a low GPA. He lost himself when he found out he hadn't been accepted. His glory days were escaping him, and his friends no longer wanted to spend time with him. They were all going off to universities, and he was stuck working a minimum-wage job at the drive-in. This deeply angered him. He became an asshole to everyone around him, pushing them further away.

But at least tonight, he could be here while everyone out there enjoyed the fair. The coach himself would be busy supervising it, so nobody would come here to question his presence. He could shower in peace and bask in the feeling of being in that locker room one last time. Or so he thought.

Then he heard the sound of footsteps, high heels clacking against the stone floor and echoing through the dimly lit room. "What the—? Is .

. . . is someone there?" Trent stumbled through his words in a drunken stupor, leaning out of the shower to see who it could be. As he stepped closer to the edge, he impaled his foot on a shard of glass that he had missed. "Damn!" His voice echoed as he hopped backward on one leg until his back hit the shower wall. He looked down at his foot; he couldn't see very well through his blurred vision, but he could tell it bled profusely. "You see what you did?" He pulled the large piece of glass from the center of his foot, causing even more blood to spill out. He left the water on while he hopped out of the shower, pulled a towel from his bag, pressed it against his foot to stop the bleeding, and noticed the footsteps had stopped. Confused, he peered around the locker room, unable to identify the culprit. "If you're here to spy on me, I hope you brought a video camera!" He stood up from the bench and tugged at his genitals, taunting whoever hid in the shadows.

BANG

A locker slammed shut on the other side of the locker room.

"That's *it*, asshole." Trent started hobbling toward the sound, nude, without a care in the world. As he passed the first row of lockers, the overhead lights flickered briefly before shutting off. He turned the corner of the final row of lockers and spotted a blurry figure seated on a bench. He rubbed his eyes to get a better look.

"Samantha?" The sun shone through the windows, highlighting her pale skin. She wore a short red bodycon dress that hugged her curves. "Wow, look at you. Way too hot in that outfit. You know I'm still shocked that you went out with Sean." Samantha stayed silent while Trent started hopping over to her. Trent stopped short when he had an epiphany. "That must've been it! You never really went missing! You were probably ditching out on that guy, huh? I always knew you were too good for him."

Samantha stood up and started walking over to him, appraising his naked body from head to toe. Trent took notice of this and got . . . *excited*.

I knew she wanted me, he thought. "So, you were just watching me shower, weren't you?" He shoved her back down onto the bench. He placed his hand on her chest and pushed her into a lying position, shoving her down harder when she tried to resist. "You know you should've just said yes when I asked you out the first time. Unless *this*—" He slid his hand beneath her skirt. "—was all you wanted."

"No!" She squirmed and tried to close her legs, blocking his access, but he only got more aggressive.

"Oh, you want it *rough* then?" With one hand, he pulled her panties down below her thighs; he used the other to spread her legs apart. He slowly pulled up her dress and noticed a change in her demeanor when they locked eyes. She smiled. "So *that's* how you like it? I always knew you'd be a freak," he said.

She reached down and gripped his shaft. Trent closed his eyes to enjoy the moment until her grip squeezed too hard, tightening and tightening until Trent screamed in pain.

"What the fuck is wrong with you?" he yelled, as he tried to shove her arm away, but she wouldn't let go. He could feel himself getting weaker every second. Once he could no longer focus on anything but the pain, she pushed him off her, causing him to crash head-first into a locker. As he gasped for air on the ground, Samantha's eyes were drawn to the bleeding wound on the bottom of his foot. She pressed her right heel into it, causing Trent to scream even more.

He crawled away as quickly as he could, but Samantha kept up with him at a slow pace, predatory and calm. When Trent stopped at a dead end, Samantha opened the locker next to where he lay and held his head in its doorway.

"No, please! I'm sorry!" Trent cried out. He started to fear the worst. If he were to die here and now, he could never fix all the mistakes he made. He would never try to get into college or play football again. He could never apologize to any of his friends who he'd taken his anger out on over the years. He would never make anybody proud of him ever again.

He looked up at Samantha, hoping she would see his pain and come to her senses, but she smirked before slamming the locker door on his head. She slammed it again and again, deaf to the screams. By the third crush, he fell unconscious, and on the fourth, his body went limp.

Trent's Phone:
I heard you were
at the fair?
Have you seen
Kyle anywhere?
—Ethan

Chapter 14

Adalynn

"Emma and the others just got here," Ethan said.

"Great." Adalynn already felt fed up with the day. She still hadn't gotten in touch with Kyle, so Ethan hoped to cheer her up by looking for him around the high school and fairgrounds. She knew he'd only made her come along in the hope that being surrounded by all of their friends while eating junk food and playing games would make her forget about the fiasco of her first date. But she wasn't interested in that. She worried about Kyle. It had been a full day since anyone had heard from him, and for some reason, no one made a big deal out of it. *Shouldn't they be more concerned after all the other disappearances?* Lucky for her, Ethan's a smart guy, and she believed he could find Kyle. He suggested they start by talking to Coach Bradley since he was the last known person to see Kyle. "Have them meet us at the dunk tank," she said.

The fair had only been open for a couple of hours, but the coach looked absolutely soaked. A high school student Adalynn vaguely recognized had just finished dunking him and walked away from the booth, leaving Coach Bradley struggling through the water to get to the ladder. Being dressed in blue jeans and a jacket didn't help matters.

"Coach!" Ethan yelled as soon as he hopped out of the tank.

"Ethan? Adalynn! How's Samantha?" he asked.

"She's good, I think. She's somewhere here at the fair, apparently," Ethan said. "By the way, have you seen Kyle?"

"Not yet! Isn't he supposed to be with you?" The coach looked at Adalynn. After a brief silence, his eyes widened with realization. "Wait, you mean you guys still haven't seen him since yesterday?"

They shook their heads.

"Okay, let me think...." Coach Bradley started pulling at his beard.

"Coach, are you gonna get back up in that chair?" one of his volunteer football players in charge of the dunk tank yelled. "People are waiting!"

"You get up in that chair! I've gotten wet enough for today," he yelled back. "All right, I'm going back to my office and see if I can find his parents' number. Maybe he is with them. If not, someone needs to let them know he is missing. Then I'm going to call the police."

"I feel like they're all distracted looking for Damien," Adalynn said.

"You mean that little boy? Cynthia's brother, right? Well, if it's the same person doing all this, odds are they could be found together," the coach reasoned. "You guys, keep your phones on, answer if I call, and do not split up." He looked at Adalynn, her frustration written on her face. "And hey, don't you worry about Kyle. You'll get your time with him when we find him. I promise. You should've seen how excited he was telling me about your date yesterday."

Her face brightened. *He really was excited,* she thought to herself. It made her feel a lot better. However, it didn't take long for her to acknowledge her even greater fear. If he wasn't dodging the date, he must've been missing and in danger.

Emma walked up with Cynthia and Sean after the coach left.

"He seemed like he was in a hurry," Emma said.

"Yeah, he hasn't seen Kyle either. He might actually be missing," Ethan said, sounding worried. "I'm gonna go look for him. You guys find Samantha, and let me know when you find her!"

"Didn't he *just* tell us not to split up?" Adalynn reminded as Ethan started walking away.

"Yep, that's why I'm leaving you with them," he said and ran off. Adalynn turned to the group, who didn't seem sure where to start in the search for Samantha.

"I'm gonna go grab a snow cone," Adalynn said.

"You just said not to split up." Cynthia rolled her eyes.

"I never said you guys couldn't come with me, but I'm hot. I need a snow cone."

"We need to be looking for Samantha!" Sean said impatiently.

"Then you go look for her! I don't care. I'm sure she's fine. Do we really have a reason to think she's missing again?"

"She doesn't have her phone on her. We don't know where she is," Sean continued.

"I lose my phone all the time! It doesn't mean I'm missing. Go find her. I'll buy a snow cone and meet you guys after, okay?"

"Whatever. Ignore her. Let's go," Cynthia said, turning away.

Emma and Sean seemed reluctant to leave Adalynn behind, but they followed.

It took her all of five minutes to find the snow cone booth, but the winding length of the line turned her off. She scanned the line for any guy who seemed vulnerable enough to let her cut in front of him in exchange for a few seconds of flirting, but then she spotted something even better. Two back from the front of the line, reading the menu on the side of the booth—which listed thirteen different flavor options—stood Samantha. She wore a form-fitting tank top, jean shorts, and a black and white flannel shirt wrapped around her waist.

"Samantha!" Adalynn called out, slipping next to her in the line. The boys behind them were too busy in conversation to realize they had been cut.

"Oh, Adalynn! Are you here with Kyle?" Samantha asked. Adalynn made a dramatic show of looking around, emphasizing that she was alone. "I'm sorry. No word from him at all?"

"Nope. Coach Bradley thinks he's missing. Ethan's out looking for him right now."

"Oh no. We'll find him. I'm sure of it. I mean, Kyle found me!"

Adalynn ignored her while she read the menu on the wall.

"What about everyone else? Did you get Sean and them to come?" Samantha asked.

"Yeah, they're actually running around looking for you right now." Adalynn didn't look away from the menu.

"Really? Well, you found me! Let's go grab them."

"Not until I get my snow cone."

"How can I help you guys?" the girl behind the register asked. She looked young, maybe a high school sophomore. Adalynn didn't recognize her.

"Can I—" Samantha started before Adalynn interrupted.

"I would like a blue raspberry! And," Adalynn looked at Samantha, "whatever she wants."

"Cherry, please," Samantha said.

Adalynn handed the girl a ten-dollar bill and threw the change into her purse.

"Thank you, Adalynn."

"Of course. Consider it my I'm-glad-you're-alive present." Adalynn smiled at her as they were handed their snow cones through the window. She felt relieved that Samantha was safe—they were friends, after all—but right now, she was also her biggest hope that Kyle was okay. "I texted Emma and told her to meet you here. She and Cynthia are on their way."

"What about you? Are you going somewhere?"

"Yes, I'm going to find Ethan and help him look for Kyle. I'm over this fair and don't want to ruin you guys' mood. You have fun!" Adalynn saw that Samantha was going to say something to try to stop her, so she turned and walked away before she could.

Adalynn's Phone:
What's up, girl?
It's Jackson. From the
football team. I saw you at the fair
and thought you looked
sexy as hell. Wanna meet
me at the kissing booth?
—Unsaved Number

Chapter 15

Ethan

The sun started to set, and Ethan still wandered, wondering what to do. He had begun his search at the football field, where he had asked some of his old teammates if they had seen Kyle around, but no luck. He searched the school halls for a while and asked any staff members he passed by, but they all scolded him for being on the school grounds after closing times.

After hours of searching, he retraced his steps from the day before. He went back to the storage closet that they found Samantha in, hoping to find some evidence that could point him in the right direction. He used his phone as a flashlight when he entered the room through the large, steel door. The room looked like it hadn't been touched since he last set foot in there, and nothing seemed unusual. He started by scanning the floor and then moved on to the shelving units. He saw nothing out of place, just various basketballs, soccer balls, footballs, gym mats, baseball bats, etc. He almost turned and gave up on his search for anything useful, when he saw it.

He had to drop to his knees and reach beneath the shelf to grab it—a cell phone. He tried turning it on, but with his luck, of course it was dead. Thinking of the fastest way to get it charged, he ran out of the closet. He had only been in there for about ten minutes, yet the darkness of the approaching night swiftly crept up on him. He entered the locker room, hoping the coach would have a phone charger somewhere in his office. Everything looked pitch-black except for the dim light of the rising moon filtering through the window.

"Hello?" Ethan called out. He still felt uncomfortable being on a high school campus, especially in a room designated for minors to shower and get dressed. When nobody responded, he thought the coast was clear to go into Coach Bradley's office until he heard somebody inside, rustling through the drawers.

A thief? He tiptoed to the door and peeked through the glass. The office looked just as dark as the locker room. He decided to pull out the Leatherman on his keychain and crack open the door. He tried his best to get a good look at the guy, but with another bit of bad luck, the door let out a loud *creak* before he had the chance. The door swung open, and Ethan found himself staring down the barrel of a pistol. On the other end of it stood Coach Bradley.

Ethan's heart had never beat so quickly. His forehead was beaded with sweat, worse than when his team was down by four with less than two minutes in a playoff game.

"Damn, Ethan! I could've blown your whole head off," the coach said, holstering his pistol in his waistline.

"Please don't." Ethan swallowed the saliva that came rushing into his mouth.

"What the hell are you doing in here? Scared the shit out of me."

"I'm still looking for Kyle. I think I found his phone, and I was hoping you would have a charger in here."

"Well, don't creep up on me like that! You gave me a damn heart attack."

"I gave *you* a heart attack? Why the hell do you have a gun?"

"Because *I'm* not gonna go missing too."

"Good point. Did you get in touch with his parents?"

"I did. Unfortunately, they haven't seen him either. I just called the police, and they are on their way. If I were you, I would enjoy the rest of the fair while you can."

"Are you sure? I mean, I want to help find him."

"Trust me. There's not much you can do that the police can't. I'll call you if they need you to answer any questions, but I'm sure we've got it. Just leave me his phone, and I'll charge it and hand it over to the police for evidence. Seriously, Ethan, thank you. You're a good friend."

Ethan nodded.

"Thank you, Coach," Ethan said. "You know, you should really turn a light on in here. That gun won't be as much help if you can't see what you're aiming at."

"I tried, but the damn lights aren't working. It doesn't matter. I'm only going to be here until the cops show up."

"Let me know as soon as you guys find him," Ethan said on his way out. The coach's words bounced around in Ethan's head, "You're a good friend." It felt good to hear them because that was all he ever wanted to be, but he wasn't sure if he really was. He felt terrible that he hadn't searched for Kyle sooner. On top of that, he wasn't sure if he would even be looking for Kyle right now if it weren't for his sister being in such a piss-poor mood. He probably wouldn't have even given it a second thought. If anything happened to Kyle, he would blame himself for not helping sooner or not doing anything more.

Then he started to think of Damien. Poor little Damien. Poor Cynthia, for that matter. He knew what it felt like having to take care of a younger sibling; he did it all the time with Adalynn, and he knew how bad it felt to see them going through something. However, he didn't know how it felt not to know where that sibling was or, even worse, that they were in trouble. He couldn't even imagine it. And he knew that it had to be worse for Cynthia; she practically raised Damien. Just having him disappear like that had to be absolutely heartbreaking.

Ethan decided that he would continue looking for them both, Kyle *and* Damien, even if the police insisted they had it handled.

He remembered the excitement in Sean's voice when he'd shown up at the hospital after Samantha had been found. He also recognized the look of hope on her father's face when he arrived. Ethan wanted nothing more than to see the faces of his missing friends' loved ones, and he refused to accept the possibility that they could be gone for good.

Ethan made his way back out to the football field, completely pitch-black. All of the people who had been standing around or sitting in the bleachers had left. He started to walk across the field, heading back toward the fairgrounds entrance. He pulled his phone out and began dialing Emma to find out where they all were when he felt a sharp pain pierce through the back of his skull. His vision faded as he fell to the ground. He could hear soft footsteps approaching on the turf, but he couldn't bring himself to speak. His final thoughts were of Adalynn, prancing through the mall parking lot after asking Kyle to take her out. He hadn't seen her that happy since they were kids and only had a moment to regret that he wouldn't be able to see it again.

Ethan's Phone:
Any luck, dude?
Let me know
if you need help.
—Sean

Chapter 16

Adalynn

Looking for Ethan served as a pretty good cover for anybody who would question what she was actually doing. "Win me a teddy bear?" Adalynn asked, fluttering her eyelashes.

"Don't you think you have enough?" said the scowling girlfriend hanging off the arm of the guy Adalynn chose to flirt with.

Adalynn looked down at her bag, which overflowed with prizes she had convinced random guys to win for her. She figured since Kyle wasn't around to make her happy, she would find another way because she was sick and tired of stressing over the situation. It had been over twenty-four hours of full-on anxiety, and she wasn't used to it. She lived a simple, carefree life where she acted as the girl who caused others stress. It was just easier that way.

"I could always use more." She smiled at the guy, who decided to walk away with his girl instead. For Adalynn, this was just the beginning of a long night. The cool breeze gave her bare arms goosebumps. Her feet were growing sore in her cheap flip-flops. Her eyeshadow started smearing across her face as she wiped away the tears that formed whenever she thought of the perfect night she was *supposed* to be having. Opposite everyone around her, she was having the absolute *worst* night of her life. Even with her blatantly poor mood, horny drunk guys would still throw themselves at her, and she liked to take advantage of it.

"You look cold, baby. Let me warm you up." An unknown man wrapped his arm around her. He reeked of alcohol and body odor, and she pushed him off as soon as she felt his damp armpit graze her shoulder. She prepared to yell out all of her frustrations at this man until she spotted the flask in his hand.

"I bet that'll warm me up faster."

The man glanced at his flask, then back to Adalynn. "Hell yeah! That's what I'm talking about!" He handed it to her, and she carefully lifted the bottom of her top to wipe the mouthpiece. She lifted it to her lips, staining the flask with her lipstick, and began chugging what tasted like straight vodka while walking away with the man's flask.

"Hey, wait a minute!" the man yelled at her, but she ignored him and kept walking.

She made her way to a churro stand, pushing a teen boy out of the way as she cut the line in front of a group of four. The cashier handed out a churro, presumably belonging to a waiting customer who had already paid, and she grabbed it before stumbling away. She finished what remained in the flask, then dumped it in a trash can. Looking up at the giant Ferris wheel before her, in awe of the beautiful light display on the ride, she teared up at the thought of being at the top with Kyle by her side.

"Fucking idiot," she said, "going missing *before* our date! I don't need a man to take me up there." Adalynn adjusted her top and stomped her way into the line. "You guys are gross," she said, glaring at the couple making out in front of her. They both responded with a dirty look before turning their heads back to each other. She let out a frustrated breath and remained quiet for the rest of the wait.

"Just you?" the ride operator asked when she sat in the Ferris wheel seat.

"Just start the fucking ride," she barked.

"Geez. Must be that time of the month," he said, rolling his eyes as he started the ride.

"Fuck off!" she yelled back, throwing one of her flip-flops and hitting him in the back of the head. As she lifted higher and higher from the ground, she closed her eyes to prevent feeling sick as her seat rocked back and forth in the open air. "That idiot." Tears began to pour from her eyes as she remembered how happy she'd been when Kyle agreed to their date. "I finally asked you, and you—" she choked, a lump forming in her throat as she wept.

Adalynn thought back to when she had first developed feelings for Kyle. He had been a friend of Ethan's throughout their childhood, and when they moved into middle school, the boys started to pay more attention to girls. When Adalynn was in sixth grade, she went to one of their football games, and she overheard some of the boys on the team teasing Kyle for having a crush on her. Adalynn hadn't been very attractive at that age. When Kyle responded, he blurted out that she was nice to him, super funny, and above all else, *he* thought she was cute. She had never experienced being crushed on before, and she liked it. She began obsessing over the feeling. She would spend the rest of her days, leading up to that very night, learning about makeup, fashion, hair, and what boys were into. She hoped that if she made herself attractive enough, maybe one day Kyle wouldn't be too embarrassed to ask her out. That day never came, but Adalynn had eventually grown confident enough in herself to make the first move. Here is the result. Alone, drunk, missing a shoe, and holding back tears at the top of a Ferris wheel. She was so distracted by her sorrow that she didn't even realize the Ferris wheel had stopped moving.

When it suddenly began its rotation again, she felt a wave of nausea from the combination of motion sickness and cheap vodka. The Ferris wheel took about ninety seconds to reach the bottom, but it felt like an eternity. The operator opened the door and let her out. His face went sour once he realized who sat inside, but she shoved him out of the way, on the verge of vomiting. She sprinted across the fairgrounds to the best of her ability wearing only one flip-flop, barged into the women's restroom, and headed to the farthest stall to vomit.

"Hello?" Adalynn called out to confirm that she was alone. Even at her lowest, she wanted to keep her public perception as high as possible. She would never let Kyle hear about this. She continued to vomit, resting her head over the toilet bowl whenever possible. After a few painful sessions, she heard a familiar voice call out.

"Are you okay in there?"

"Who's there?" Suddenly aware of her current state, she felt disgusted with herself. Her mouth tasted like acidic churros and alcohol, and the toilet bowl in front of her smelled even worse.

"It's just me, Samantha."

Adalynn sensed her entering the stall from behind, but she was embarrassed to turn around. *Great*, she thought. "It's not fair," Adalynn said. "You got to go on your date with Sean. I mean, sure, you disappeared, but Kyle goes and disappears before our date even happened. After everything I've done to get here, this is how it turns out. It just wasn't meant to be, I guess." Adalynn tried her best not to cry. She felt Samantha step closer to her and pull Adalynn's hair out of her face as she lifted her head and vomited some more. "Thank you," Adalynn said, taking notice of the shoes that Samantha wore—red high heels. "Hey, aren't those—" Adalynn tried turning around, but Samantha's grip on her hair tightened. "Aren't those shoes the ones I lost yesterday?"

Adalynn grabbed Samantha's wrist and turned all the way around. Samantha wore the same red dress Adalynn had lost as well. As Adalynn drunkenly collected her thoughts, Samantha tilted her head, a psychotic smile plastered on her face. She closed the bathroom stall door and grabbed Adalynn by the face. Adalynn screamed and kicked at Samantha with her last remaining flip-flop. Her screams were muffled through

Samantha's palm, and she started to gasp for air. She landed a successful kick to Samantha's stomach, causing her grip to loosen for a fleeting moment. Adalynn took a deep breath while she reached for the stall door, but she slid on a pool of vomit and hit her head on the ceramic toilet bowl.

Is this really it? I spent my whole life trying to please one guy, and now it ends with me covered in vomit, blood, and toilet water. She felt a headache rising as her vision blurred red from the bleeding head wound. She thought back to how excited she had been for tonight and how ironic this would be if it were the end of her life. She closed her eyes and pictured herself atop the Ferris wheel, leaning on Kyle's shoulders, content and happy. This left her with one last beautiful smile as her consciousness faded.

Adalynn's Phone:
Hey girl, where
are you?
We should meet
up and enjoy the fair
while we're here!
—Samantha

Chapter 17

Emma

"You know, every time I see you, you're with more women than the last time. Right on!" Sean's roommate, Curtis, said, sitting beside him. Samantha, Cynthia, Sean, and Emma were taking a break from wandering the fair and were seated atop a concrete wall surrounding a planted tree. Beneath the giant Ferris wheel that illuminated the night sky, this was the nicest ambiance the fair had to offer,

"Is that something I should worry about?" Samantha asked, smiling as she wrapped her arms around Sean. Emma began to worry because Curtis had seen the two of them in a compromising position the night before, and he wasn't the smartest guy around. He could easily say something that might give Samantha the wrong idea. Emma knew that Sean harbored similar worries the moment the two of them exchanged looks.

"Only if you're the jealous type," Curtis replied, giving Sean a playful punch on the shoulder. He seemed to notice how uncomfortable Sean and Emma were with the topic and raised an eyebrow but also changed the topic. "So, Samantha. How was it being abducted?"

"Oh, you were serious about that?" Samantha looked at Sean and giggled before turning back to Curtis. "Sean told me you said that, but I thought he was just joking."

"I told ya," Sean said.

"What, you don't believe me?" Curtis looked at Emma and Cynthia. "What about you guys? Don't you think it makes sense?"

"Aliens?" Cynthia gritted her teeth.

Emma had such a nice day with her friends that she had almost forgotten about Damien.

"Dude, stop," Sean said to Curtis.

"No, it's fine. I want to hear what he has to say," Cynthia said. "If aliens are abducting people out here, did it happen to Damien too?"

Curtis's eyes widened in fear of Cynthia. Apparently, he had also forgotten about Damien. "No, I'm sorry. I didn't mean it."

"Don't do that. I want to hear your little theory. If aliens took him, what do you think they're doing to him?"

"Promise you won't hurt me?"

"Dude, she's not gonna hurt you," Sean said.

Curtis swallowed. He's clearly high out of his mind, but it still made Emma uncomfortable, seeing a guy afraid of Cynthia like this.

"Okay then. When it comes to aliens, we first have to ask ourselves, *why*? If they were so far advanced with technology to have developed the level of space travel required to reach Earth, *why* would they want to?"

"To kill us?" Samantha asked.

"That's what the movies would have you think, but I don't believe it. That just doesn't make sense."

"To research us?" Sean offered.

"Now, that makes more sense. If we found alien life, we most certainly would make researching them our priority. But I don't believe that applies in this case either."

"What? Why not?" Cynthia asked.

"Because there have been reports of alien sightings and abductions for *years, decades*, even. Think about it. Lubbock, Roswell, hell, it goes all the way back to ancient Egyptians writing about them with hieroglyphs.

My point is, they've been here long enough to be done researching us by now."

"So, why *would* they be here?" Emma asked.

Curtis leaned in. "What do we do when we run out of resources to survive on Earth? Our population is rapidly growing, and the climate is constantly changing. It's only a matter of time until we can't inhabit the Earth anymore. So, what then?"

"We leave," Samantha said.

"Ding ding ding. You got it. We go to another planet and make it livable for ourselves."

"So, you think that's what they're here for? To kill us all and take the planet for themselves." Cynthia said.

"I didn't say anything about killing us. No, that's not their goal. It's *replacing* us."

"Wouldn't that mean killing us?" Cynthia asked.

"Not all of us," Curtis said. "I believe that they would like to coexist with us. Killing all of us would be too difficult. Sure, with their technology, they probably have better weapons than us, but it would be hard to transport a large enough quantity of them *and* sufficient forces for a full-scale war. And that war would likely ruin the planet, which would be counterproductive to them. So, coexisting would be their best option."

"Then, why are they still abducting people?" Samantha asked.

"Good question. They know humans wouldn't trust them if they just showed up on Earth. There's no way we would let them just live here. So they had to devise another way to live with us."

"And what would that be *exactly*?" Cynthia asked.

"Like I said before, by *replacing* us. They would have the technology to do it. Abduct a person at random and *become* them. Study their DNA, replace it with their own, and take that person's place here on Earth," Curtis said.

Everyone just stared at him blankly.

Sean broke the silence. "Well, now you've officially lost me."

"Yeah, honestly. You sounded smart for a few minutes, but you dove off the deep end with that last bit."

"I don't think so," Curtis insisted. "You have to realize that this would be a species *far* more advanced than we are. Technologically, medically, intelligently, you name it."

"So what about Samantha, then?" Cynthia asked.

"What about me?"

"What do you think happened to her? Do you think she was replaced?"

"Oh, most certainly," Curtis said. "Don't get me wrong. You don't have to believe any of this, but a girl disappears without a trace for a few days and returns with no memory, injuries, or signs of sexual abuse? Yeah, she got abducted. And there would've been no other logical reason for her to be here alive right now."

Sean slapped his forehead in embarrassment. "Samantha, I'm sorry. We don't have to keep listening—"

She interrupted him. "So, let's say you're right. What if I *am* an alien? You don't seem too scared of me right now. Wouldn't a conspiracy theorist like *you* avoid me at all costs?" Everyone looked at Samantha in shock, surprised at how well she took all of this, let alone wanting to keep the conversation rolling.

"Not at all. I think your goal is ultimately to coexist with us. I don't think you're a threat, and at the end of the day, as long as you still pretend to be the Samantha we all know and love and treat my Sean nicely, I have nothing to fear."

"So why me?" Samantha asked. "And why Damien?"

"Bad luck? We are a small enough town, probably just out of sight enough for major governments not to take the disappearances too seriously."

"Okay, and why Earth? If they were trying to get to a better place to live, why would they go to one with a short shelf life due to climate change, disease, and wars?" Samantha asked.

"Plenty of reasons. It could just be the only other safe planet out there. Or, they could believe that they are advanced enough to fix our issues. Once they get enough of their own on our planet, they will start replacing politicians and ending wars. Their planet will have exhausted more resources than us by now, and they could have the knowledge to keep ours alive. It's too hard to pin down one reason, but the reasons are there," Curtis said.

Emma could feel herself dozing off, finally feeling the anxiety of her friends being missing and the fatigue from hours of running around the fair catching up with her.

"Woah, Emma, are you okay? You look like you're going to fall asleep," Cynthia said.

"Yeah, this conversation is exhausting." Emma stood up. "I'm gonna go wash my face." She went to the restroom nearest the Ferris wheel, which seemed empty. She turned the sink on and splashed her face a few times when she heard the stall in the back open up. Emma looked in the mirror and thought her eyes must be playing tricks on her. Samantha walked out of the stall and passed her. Something seemed different, though. She wore a red dress and must have had heels on since she stood significantly taller than Emma was used to. Plus, her hair looked like she had straightened it, but Emma recalled her hair being in a curly bun.

Did she walk in behind me? Emma thought. *And wasn't she wearing a flannel shirt and shorts?* Emma ran out of the bathroom to follow her, but she'd vanished from sight. She took notice of another girl wearing a similar red dress, but she had blonde hair. *Are my eyes just playing tricks on me?*

She went back to her friends, who were still joking around with Curtis on the topic of aliens. She began second-guessing herself because she felt so exhausted she ultimately couldn't be sure if she should ask. She didn't want anyone to think she was crazy.

"Curtis . . ." she interrupted him, unsure of what he had even been talking about before. "Could there be any chance that the alien could've taken Samantha's appearance and still kept the real one alive?"

"What do you mean?" he asked.

"Would you say it's possible that this *is* the real Samantha, and the alien could still be out there taking on her appearance?"

"I suppose it *could* be possible. I don't think it's likely, though. It would be too much risk for the alien. What if the two of them encountered each other? It would blow the alien's cover. It would make more sense just to kill the person and take their place."

Emma looked to Cynthia, who she expected to be upset at hearing him talk about Damien being potentially killed, but she felt relieved that she didn't take any of what he said seriously.

"Emma, where's this coming from?" Sean asked.

"No, it's nothing. I'm just tired, is all," Emma said.

"What's that supposed to mean?"

"My eyes must have been playing tricks on me, I don't know," Emma said, taking notice of a kid or two running past them in the direction of the football field. "I just thought I saw Samantha a second ago."

"Duh, I'm right here," Samantha said. Now, a whole group of kids were running toward the field.

"No, I mean in the bathroom. I thought I saw you in there, but you were in this really pretty dress."

"Wow, Sean. You've got your girls daydreaming about each other," Curtis said.

Sean ignored his comment.

"Okay, Emma. You're right. You're probably just tired. We should get you back home. I mean, it *is* pretty late—" A man sprinting past them interrupted Sean by bumping into him, moving in the same direction as the rest of the crowd. "What the hell?" Sean stood and looked to see where everyone was going. "Uh, you guys?"

They all gave him their attention.

"There are a bunch of cops on the football field," he said.

Emma's Phone:
Hey, honey, I heard
about Damien. Is
Cynthia okay?
Tell her I'm
here if she needs
anything.
—Mom

Chapter 18

Cynthia

"I heard they found a body!" a voice called out from the group of jocks running by.

"Do you think it's Kyle?" another voice rang out.

"Oh my God, did they just say Kyle?" Emma asked.

"I think so. Come on. We should go check it out," Sean said.

"No, sir. Not me," said Curtis. "Cops and dead bodies aren't my thing. It's probably best if we all just get out of here."

"You know we can't do that. If that's Kyle, we need to know," Sean insisted.

"Suit yourselves. I'm going home." Curtis ran off in the opposite direction while the four of them followed the crowd to the flashing police lights surrounding the football field. Caution tape blocked off at least half of the field. They had to shove their way through the massive crowd of other curious onlookers.

"That's not Kyle," Cynthia confirmed since she stood taller than the rest of them.

On the field were two standard police cars and a large black SUV. The three vehicles formed a triangle around a body covered by a white tarp, which lay directly on top of the school's logo on the fifty-yard line. Alongside two police officers was the same investigator on Damien's missing person case, dressed in an all-black suit and sunglasses even though it was nighttime. Cynthia recognized him from her house. There were another two police officers in charge of crowd control along the caution tape barriers.

"I agree," Sean said.

"What, how do you know?" Samantha asked.

"Kyle's bigger than that," Sean said.

"Yeah, and if he were there this whole time, somebody would've seen him before now. Whoever this is, it had to have *just* happened," Cynthia said.

"Oh my God," Emma said suddenly. "We need to call Ethan and Adalynn. Make sure they're okay."

"Right. I'll call Adalynn," Samantha said. "Emma, call Ethan."

"I'm already on it," Emma said. Cynthia's chest tightened when she saw it. She didn't want it to be real. The police near the body turned as the phone lit up on the field.

"No," Sean said. The police grabbed the phone, and Cynthia watched as they declined the incoming call.

"Ethan didn't answer," Emma said. "What?" Cynthia and Sean's eyes were both wide with fear. They weren't sure what to say, but they both knew.

"Call him again," Sean said. Cynthia thought the same thing, too afraid to see what would happen. Emma redialed, and the phone lit up in the police officer's hands again. This time, Emma saw it and understood what it meant.

"No!" She began to scream and cry as she tried to run out on the field to him. The police officer standing guard immediately blocked her. "That's my friend out there!"

"That's even more of a reason for you to stay back," the officer assured her.

"Yeah, kid. You don't want to see him like that," his partner added.

"Emma, come on!" Sean said. "We need to let the officers do their job."

"But, it's... Etha—" She couldn't finish saying his name.

"I know, I know. But whoever did this... We need to let the cops find them," Sean said.

Cynthia had a hard time watching. She didn't want to believe that something had happened to *any* of her friends. She began to worry about Damien obsessively. *It has got to be unrelated*, she thought, unable to convince herself. She turned around to hide her tears from her friends, who were all going through similar emotions. As she dried her eyes, she saw her near the far back of the crowd.

"Sean?" Cynthia said through a sniffle.

"Emma, come on, please!" Sean yelled.

"Sean!" Cynthia repeated.

"What?" he turned around, frustrated.

Cynthia pointed to her. She stood tall in a red dress and high heels, her hair straight, without a single negative emotion on her face. It was Samantha. Or at least, it looked like her. Cynthia looked to her side to confirm that the Samantha she had spent the day with stood next to her, and Sean did the same. Their Samantha looked even more confused than Cynthia did.

Cynthia looked back toward the doppelganger, and they locked eyes before she turned and walked away from the crowd. Cynthia, Samantha, and Sean looked at each other and knew they all thought the same thing. *Was Curtis right?* Cynthia led the way as they began pushing through the crowd after her.

"Sean!" a voice called out from the crowd. It was Coach Bradley. "What's going on?"

"Coach, I'm sorry. It's Ethan out there," Sean said, "Please, go make sure Emma's okay, then come and find us." He tilted his head toward Emma, being comforted in the police officer's arms while the crowd watched, some of them with their phone cameras out. Coach Bradley nodded.

Samantha's double, whoever she was, moved like the fastest walker Cynthia had ever seen. She seemed to be walking at an average pace, but the amount of ground she had covered in such a short time didn't make any sense. They spotted her at the entrance to the fair's Hall of Mirrors. The opening of the building featured a giant green alien head with its mouth wide open for you to walk through. She looked at them and gave a devious smile before entering.

"You've got to be fucking kidding me," Sean said. "Did anyone else see that smile? She's up to something. That was the look of a psychopath."

"Yeah, I don't really feel comfortable chasing her in there. Shouldn't we go get the police?" Samantha asked.

"No. We'll lose her. I have to go in." Cynthia moved with determination. She knew that whoever this was, she existed as the cause of all of their problems. Ethan's death. Kyle's disappearance. Damien.

"She's right," Sean said.

Cynthia motioned for them to follow her as she entered the building.

"God, this feels like we're in a horror movie," Samantha said. Mirrors filled the room from wall to wall while ominous music played in the background—the kind of music you would hear in an early alien film. The three of them began traversing the maze; some of the walls were set on timers that would rotate the mirrors, opening and closing the walkways.

"Seriously, fuck this," Sean said. "How are we supposed to find her in here? She's probably left by now!"

"No. You saw how she smiled at us. She's playing games with us. She's definitely still here," Cynthia said. The mirror to her right moved, revealing a new entrance. Straight across, she saw Samantha. "There!" She made a run for her, only to run straight into what was actually another mirror. She cracked the glass as she ran into it, leaving minor cuts across her forehead.

"Are you okay?" Samantha cried.

"Yeah. Sean!" Cynthia yelled as she saw the dress-wearing Samantha quickly walking up behind him before being blocked by a moving mirror. The mirror rotated in front of Sean, dividing him from the rest of the group.

"Shit!" Samantha ran to the mirror and banged on it. "Sean! Can you hear me?" No response.

"Quit banging on it, or you'll end up like me," Cynthia said, blood trickling down her face. "Come on, by the time that one moves, they'll be gone. We need to keep moving and see if we can run into them somewhere else."

"Let's just hurry."

The two of them ran through the hallways without direction, catching occasional glimpses of an unconscious Sean being dragged by the hair through the mirrors. Cynthia saw that Samantha had run out of energy but knew they had to continue. Cynthia needed answers, and she couldn't let Sean die too. They found themselves in an octagonal room they assumed functioned as the center of the building. The walls around them were constantly spinning, allowing multiple options for entry.

"Where do we go next?" Samantha jumped at the sound of glass shattering behind them.

Cynthia looked in the direction of the sound and saw that Samantha's double had shattered a mirror and now held a large shard of glass to Sean's throat. Her hand bled freely from gripping the glass.

"Who are you? What the fuck do you want? Why do you *look* like me?" Samantha yelled.

"Where's Damien?" Cynthia asked, keeping her voice calm.

She only smiled and pressed the glass closer to Sean's throat, breaking the skin.

"Sean!" Samantha screamed with tears in her eyes.

He finally woke up and looked down to see the glass pressing into his skin. His eyes widened, and he struggled, pulling on the hand gripping his hair. The heel of her right shoe snapped suddenly, and she fell to the floor. Sean tried to jump on top of her but slipped on the blood from her hand pooled on the floor.

"No!" Samantha screamed as Sean fell onto the glass fragment held by the double. He gasped violently for air the moment it entered his rib cage.

Cynthia and Samantha rushed to his aid, but the doppelganger had gotten to her feet first and held Sean by the head with both hands, threatening to press her thumbs into his eyes.

They were begging her not to do it when they heard a loud *bang* that echoed through the building. The look-alike dropped to the floor with Sean, still struggling to breathe. Samantha immediately ran to his side and applied pressure to his wound. Behind the rotating wall, Cynthia noticed a figure approaching.

Coach Bradley entered the room with Emma. She dropped to the floor at Sean's side and tried speaking to him, but her words were incomprehensible through her tears.

"Coach! Thank God," Cynthia said. Then she saw the gun in his right hand. And heard the single shot.

"I'm sorry I took so long. This maze was difficult as hell to get through," he said.

Cynthia didn't recognize the man who entered the room behind him, although the suit he wore looked similar to the one Damien's investigator had been wearing.

"He needs medical treatment. I'll carry him out and rush him to the hospital," the man said.

Samantha peered up at him, reluctant to remove her hand. "How are you going to get him out of here?" she asked. Just as she said it, the mirrors stopped rotating.

"I ordered that this place be shut down. The exit is this way. Now, do you want to ask more questions, or do you want your friend to live?"

Samantha nodded.

Coach Bradley helped lift Sean onto the man's shoulders, and they all followed him to the exit.

"You know, it would've been helpful if you hadn't killed her," Cynthia said. "Now we can't ask her where my little brother is."

"I'm sorry, but I didn't see any other option," Coach Bradley said. "I wasn't going to let her kill Sean."

"I know, it just sucks," Cynthia said. She had stayed strong for the night, but now that things were starting to feel over, she worried Damien would be gone for good. She wouldn't get the closure she had hoped for throughout this nightmare.

Cynthia's Phone:
Hey, is Samantha still with you? This is her dad. She hasn't come home yet. I'm just worried. Have her call me.
—Mr. Roberts

Chapter 19

Samantha

"She's in there," the suited man told his partners, who waited for them at the exit. They quickly ran into the Hall of Mirrors. Samantha and the group followed the suited man carrying Sean to the parking lot, where they loaded him into the back of one of their black SUVs. Samantha noticed that the fair had been cleared, not because of the late hour but because it was an active crime scene. They all watched as the SUV drove off with Sean.

"Feel better!" Samantha yelled at the car, hoping Sean could hear her.

"He's gonna be okay, right?" Emma asked.

"Yes, of course. Nobody could get him help any faster. And he was still breathing, so his lungs weren't pierced. He was very lucky," another suited man said. "Now, I know you guys have had a really long and stressful night, but we need to ask you all some questions. We need to understand what happened here tonight."

"Absolutely not," Cynthia said. "I'm sick of this. I'm sick of all of these questions. I'm sick of my friends going missing, being attacked, *dying*... It's too much. We've answered your questions before, and you still haven't found my little brother. Things have only gotten worse! Fuck all of this."

"Cynthia, right?" the man clarified. "I'm sorry. We can't control everything. We are still doing our best to find your brother, but we're going to need your help to make it happen. Please."

"You know where I live. That bitch in there is dead now, so Damien can't be in any more trouble—if he's even still alive. I'm going home, and I'm going to sleep. I am *exhausted*. If you still need questions answered, find me in the morning. Come on, Emma." Cynthia wrapped an arm around her and walked off before the man could respond.

"Samantha, are you coming too?" Emma asked.

"I think I'll stay. Someone needs to tell them what happened. I still have my dad's truck, so don't worry about me," she said.

Emma nodded and walked Cynthia to her car.

"So, I just have a few questions for you, Samantha, starting with the events of your disappearance and leading up to now." A suited man spoke to her as she leaned against his SUV in the parking lot. Coach Bradley was also being interviewed by a separate man a few parking spaces down.

"Yes, of course. Anything," she said.

"It is our understanding that you do not recall *any* of the events that transpired from when you disappeared until yesterday. Is that correct?"

"Yes. One minute, I'm in Sean's car and the next minute, I'm waking up in a hospital bed." Samantha rubbed her arms as a cool breeze kicked in. Her flannel shirt helped keep her warm, but her thighs started getting goosebumps.

"Interesting," the man said, pulling his notebook from the back pocket of his suit pants as he started jotting things down.

"So this Sean, you're sure he was not involved in your disappearance?"

"Of course not!"

"No need to get worked up. We just have to check everything. Make sure all the stories add up. Where is Sean now?"

"One of your guys just took him to the hospital. That girl in there attacked him."

"The one they say looks just like you?"

"Yes. Do you know who she is?"

"Unfortunately, it's classified. I cannot disclose that to you."

"Classified? What the hell does that mean? This girl that looks just like me attacks my friends, and I can't even know who she is?"

"Leave the questions to me," he said, his tone smooth and crisp, brooking no dissent. "Now, who else was with you tonight? Who else knew what happened here?"

"It was just me, Sean, Emma, Cynthia, and the coach. Ethan was here, but he..."

"It's okay. You don't have to say it. Was there anybody else?"

"Ethan's little sister was here too. Oh God, Adalynn! I haven't seen her in hours! She probably doesn't know about Ethan yet. I need to call her." Samantha started reaching for her phone but quickly realized she didn't have it.

"Don't worry. We will let his family know. Was that everybody?"

"I think so," Samantha said.

The man finished writing in his notepad and closed it up. "Would you excuse me for a moment?" he asked, and she nodded. The man walked to the coach, nodding at another pair of men in suits, who jumped in their SUV and peeled out of the parking lot. The man whispered something in the ear of the investigator interrogating the coach, and he nodded. Samantha overheard the man's next question for the coach.

"You mentioned some sort of mess in your locker room. Elaborate."

"Yes, sir. A locker was destroyed, and I think I saw blood there," Coach Bradley said.

"Would you mind showing me?"

The coach agreed and started heading for the locker room. Samantha let out a high-pitched scream as she watched the man who had interrogated her pull out a pistol and, without hesitation, shoot Coach Bradley in the back of the head.

Chapter 20

Emma

"It still doesn't feel real," Emma said, rubbing her eyes as she struggled to drive through her exhaustion and emotional turmoil.

"What part?"

"All of it. Ethan, that Samantha look-alike, Sean being stabbed..." Emma forced herself to stop listing things. "It just doesn't feel real. I mean, what even was that... that *thing*? She looked just like Samantha. I mean, was Curtis on to something?"

"No way. I refuse to write off tonight as fucking *aliens*. Not my Damien. I won't let him get wrapped up in these conspiracies. He deserves to be found. Whoever that was, was just some freak stalker. She probably was obsessed with Samantha and thought it best to attack all of her friends."

"Then why Damien?"

"Because Samantha knew him? I don't know. Not every psychopath has logical thought processes. In fact, I'm sure most of them don't."

"You're right. I'm sorry," Emma said as she pulled into Cynthia's empty driveway.

"Go get some rest, and we will find Damien. I promise."

"I know. Thank you." Cynthia closed the door, and Samantha watched until she entered her house.

I should call Adalynn, Emma thought as she pulled her car out of the driveway. She listened to the rings for an answer that never came. So she left a voicemail. "Hey, Adalynn, it's Emma. I'm assuming you're probably home asleep right now, but . . . just give me a call when you can." *She's gonna have the worst day of her life tomorrow.* Emma thought about how Adalynn and her parents would react to the news of Ethan's passing. *At least the bitch that did it is dead.*

Emma wanted to head to the hospital to check on Sean but felt herself dozing off behind the steering wheel. *I should just go home,* she told herself at the stop sign. Rather than making a right turn, she continued straight through. Then she suddenly felt an immense pressure coming from the passenger side of the vehicle, and almost as if gravity had flipped itself over at that moment, her car now veered upside down. She felt stinging pain as she watched blood flow from cuts all over her body. Glass from the windows had shredded her skin on impact. She unbuckled her seat belt and dropped to the floor. She had to crawl over broken glass to squeeze herself out of where her front windshield had been. Panic set in when she tried to stand but couldn't feel her legs. *Oh my God,* she thought, rolling onto her back and working up the courage to look down at the damage. She felt a short sense of relief that her legs were still there, but the panic came back when she tried to wiggle her toes and couldn't.

"Fuck!" she screamed, not from pain, but terror. Her voice carried loudly through the suburban neighborhood. She heard footsteps approaching from behind her car, now set ablaze.

With relief, she saw one of the suited men who had helped Sean to the hospital.

"Oh, thank God! Please, you've gotta help me! I can't feel my legs," she cried out. *Wait, why does he have a gun? Is he pointing it at me?*

Emma's Phone:
Thanks for the ride.

I'll call you in the morning.
—Cynthia

Samantha

Samantha's body filled with shock as she watched Coach Bradley fall to the floor. She stood there beside the SUV, numb and silent, until the same man turned and pointed his gun at her. After feeling the vibration of the bullet that hit the SUV ricochet beside her, she ran for the trees on the outskirts of the parking lot. As soon as she entered the woods, she fell down a small hill and received multiple cuts to her bare legs. She took a moment to assess the damage, noticed her clothes had been torn in several places, and began running through the woods again as soon as she heard voices from atop the hill. She figured she could gain some distance and ran as quickly as she could while they carefully walked down the hill. She would occasionally trip over sticks and rocks in her path, but only once did she actually fall to the ground. Splayed out, she took a quick second to mentally acknowledge all the times she'd made fun of the girl in horror movies who would fall while being chased, then got up and kept running.

My truck is back in the parking lot, she thought to herself. *There's no way I can go back to it.* She would hide in bushes and behind trees to catch her breath and check to see how far behind the men were.

"She couldn't have gotten far!" one man said.

"How could we lose some little girl?" she heard from another. Rather than taking offense at the statement, she felt a sense of pride that she made it difficult for them to catch her.

"The boss is going to kill us. He said no witnesses."

"If the public finds out what's going on here, it's gonna be all bad."

"We can't let that happen."

What exactly is going on here? Samantha couldn't help but think back to Curtis's theories. *Was he actually right all along?*

The suited men chased Samantha to an opening deep in the woods, a large, circle-shaped clearing surrounded by trees. The two men cautiously walked toward the center of the circle, where mixed looks of shock, disbelief, confusion, and even a fair bit of excitement lit up their faces.

"No way," one of them said as he bent down to pick up the flannel shirt. The other man kicked the pile of clothes that lay in the middle of the clearing. Everything that Samantha had worn that evening—her shoes, top, shorts, and even her underwear—sat empty before them. Samantha was nowhere to be seen.

Epilogue

Cynthia

Cynthia awoke in a cold sweat. She had been having nightmares about the events from the night before. She dreamt of Ethan being attacked by Samantha's look-alike, followed by attacks on Sean, Emma, and Samantha. She watched as Coach Bradley missed his shot before she slit his throat. And right before that same glass shard could reach her own throat, she woke up and found herself on the couch in her living room.

She walked to the fridge and poured herself a glass of water. As she sipped it, she glanced at the clock above the stove; it read 3:29 a.m. *I couldn't even sleep through the night,* she thought.

Knock Knock Knock

The sound frightened Cynthia enough for her to jump and spill her water. *It's the middle of the night!* She slowly approached the door and tried to look through the peephole, but nobody was there. *Maybe they went away*, she thought, but she heard it again as she prepared to walk up the stairs.

Knock Knock Knock

She jumped enough to drop the glass on the carpeted stairs this time. "Fuck this!" she said aloud as she charged up to the door and swung it open. She didn't see anybody at first until she looked down.

"Damien?"

Also By Matthew Mercer

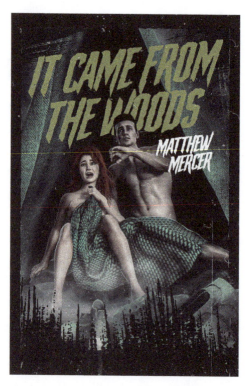

They agreed to make a documentary. They didn't know it was about their own massacre. Now, Nancy Miller is faced with the impossible task of proving to the world that Bigfoot killed her friends.

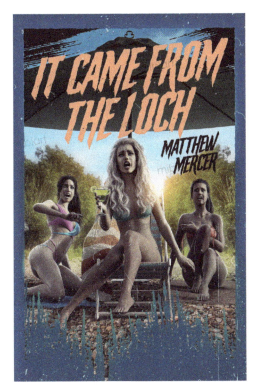

Her family died on the loch, now it's her job to study it. Decades after a tragic accident left Elizabeth an orphan, she is making her return with her friends and daughter. Will she find the answers she has been looking for her whole life, or will history repeat itself?

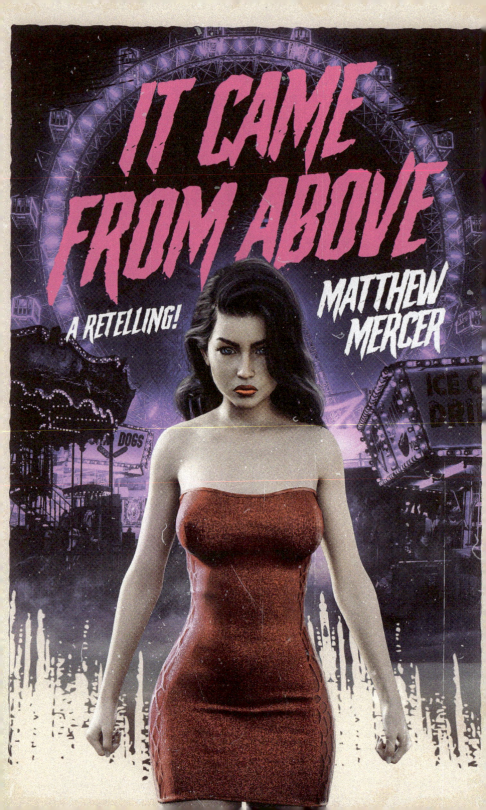

For Dobby

It Came From Above: A Retelling!

My heart raced from the moment I woke up that morning. I jumped out of bed and into the shower, singing along with every song from my phone speaker, which I set to my most upbeat Spotify playlist. I hummed and danced along while I brushed my teeth—a job made easier by my uncontrollable smile. The singing and dancing continued while I finished my morning routine:

- Drying my hair

- Brushing it

- Putting clothes on

- Eating cereal at the table with my dad while he scrolled through the local news on his phone.

Once I finished eating, I rushed him into the car so he could take me to the nail salon. I wanted to get them done the day before, but I thought they'd look nicer if I did it today. I should've made an appointment, which I realized too late because this wasn't something that I often did. But, it was a special occasion. My dad was right; the nail salon took forever, and by the time I got home, I was rushing to finish getting ready. I still had to straighten my hair, pick a matching pair of underwear he might like (not that I was planning for him to see them), put on makeup, pick out a dress, and spray on my favorite perfume.

When I heard his car horn outside, my heart skipped a beat. Until now, all I felt was excitement for this date, but now that he was here, the nervousness set in. I looked toward the medicine cabinet on the bathroom wall. Inside was my bottle of depression/anxiety pills prescribed by my doctor after my mom died. They helped me when I needed them, but I never liked the *feeling* of needing them. I wanted to be normal and happy like everyone else without being constantly medicated. I would always tell myself that I'd be fine without them, but I couldn't deny that they calmed my nerves at times like this, and I wasn't going to let *anything* ruin tonight, especially not myself. I walked to my bathroom and opened the medicine cabinet.

What if he ends up not liking me? Did I prepare enough? Did I remember to shave? Put on deodorant? What if he thinks I'm boring? What if this is all just a big prank? I stopped and took a deep breath. Sean wasn't like that. He is a nice guy, and we've been close friends for years. To top it off, our friends often told me of how big a crush he's had on me this entire time—I just never believed them. Once he *did* ask me on this date, I was overflowing with joy. *How lucky was I to have someone as great as him interested in me?*

I took the pills from the cabinet, popped open the container, and swallowed two with a handful of water from the sink. Then I returned to my bedroom and looked at the last two pairs of shoes I set on my bed, struggling to choose. My options were open-toed, wedge, dress sandals, or basic black flip-flops. Sean honked his horn, so I hurried my decision-making. The wedges made me feel classier and seemed more fitting for the occasion, but I knew the date was for a drive-in movie, and they would probably be coming off. Plus, Sean would want me to be comfortable and wouldn't likely spend too much time staring at my feet, so I grabbed the flip-flops and slipped them on.

He honked his horn again, so I waved goodbye to my dad and hurriedly left my house. I carried my nervousness as a weight in my chest that tried to escape my body in the form of goosebumps as soon as I sat in his car. He dressed nicer than I was used to seeing him: khaki pants and a black dress shirt. Once I saw the way he looked at me, I had no reason to be nervous. He felt the same way about me as I did him.

He drove us to the theater, and we enjoyed each other's company along the way. My uncontrollable smile transitioned to an uncontrollable giggle that came out with everything he said. My face was hurting from my perma-grin. Everything went great. Time flew by and we were both happy, even through the awkward encounter with Trent at the ticket booth. When his car and radio started to act up, I thought it was cute how he looked confused, embarrassed, and eventually scared once the rest of the drive-in's electricity went haywire.

He offered to get us some snacks and left me with the task of finding which radio station we were supposed to play to hear the movie, but my mind was elsewhere. It wasn't what I had planned when I agreed to come with him on this date, and it certainly wasn't the setting where I imagined my first time would take place, but the time felt right, and to say I was excited would be an understatement.

How about I just tease him and see where it goes? I reached under my dress, grabbed my panties, and slid them down my legs. I knew Sean would be out of sight soon, so I quickly yanked them off. *At least he didn't see that.* I used the hand crank to roll the window down and whistled as loud as I could, watching him in the side mirror. When he looked back, I held my arm out, fist facing upward, opened my hand, and let the panties unroll and hang from my index and middle fingers. *That was sexy, right?* I thought so before doing it, but now that it was happening, I only felt embarrassment, at least, until he walked straight into the trash can. *I guess that means he liked it.*

I laughed harder than I ever had in my entire life. Sean made me feel good like this, even when he wasn't trying. This let me know that no matter what I did, I couldn't ruin this date.

Tonight might be the night! My virginity wasn't something I was exactly saving for the right person, but it was something I wanted to remember and not regret. Of all the people in this town, Sean would be the last person I would regret, and a drive-in movie theater's parking lot would *definitely* be something I remembered. I made it my personal goal to give him an experience worth remembering. *Just wait until you get back. This is going to be life-changing.*

I reached for the radio dial to search for the proper channel as he instructed, and the lights on the display flickered again. I wasn't scared when it happened the first time, and I didn't think I was this time, but my breath fell short. My chest felt heavy. My stomach dropped like I had gone through a loop on a high-speed roller coaster. My vision blurred, and I struggled to finish a single thought. Then, I woke up.

My head hurt when I woke up—this was totally new for me. It came from experiencing a lifetime of memories rushing through my brain over the course of an hour. I opened my mouth and took three deep breaths to get used to the sensation. The transformation was complete.

I felt a rush of cold air graze across my new body as the door to the surgical pod opened. I tried to open my eyes, but the bright white lights in my ship were far too much for a human to handle.

This will take a lot of getting used to. With a single mental note, I commanded my ship—as humans would call it—to dim the lights until my eyes could open without stress.

Back on my home planet, we have access to elements unknown to Earth's periodic table—a term I'm just learning. Thanks to this, as you might expect, we have technology far more advanced than humans could ever conceive. A perfect example of this would be my ship, for lack of a better term. I suppose UFO would also work, but a spaceship just sounds silly. I'm gonna go with ship. Where I'm from, we don't have words as humans do. We do all of our communication emotionally and mentally. You might call it telepathy, but it's not exactly the same. Regardless, using this method of communication, my ship and I are connected consciously. All I need to do is think of what I need, and it provides it for me.

Getting a feel for my new body, I started with what felt most natural. I wiggled my fingers and curled my toes. Once I got used to that, I clenched and unclenched my fists. Then I rotated my ankles. I turned my head to the side and was greeted with my first sense of claustrophobia from the narrow walls of the surgical pod. I turned my head back to face this ship's plain, white ceiling through the open door to the pod. I held my hands in front of my face and continued to play with them, watching as I got used to the motions. I looked down toward my feet and continued testing my ankle and toe muscles before I examined the rest of my new body.

My breasts sunk into my chest, as I learned they do when women lie on their backs like this. The pink coloration of my nipples, in contrast with the rest of my otherwise pale skin, intrigued me. I ran my hand over them. *Soft.* I took my right index finger and pressed my left nipple into my breast, watching with peculiarity as it hardened. It was a pleasurable feeling that somehow left me embarrassed. Human emotions are weird, and it would take a while for me to get used to them.

I should leave that alone for now.

I brought my attention back down to my feet and took turns straightening each leg, one at a time, bending them at the knee. When they reached their full extension, I rotated my ankles around again. I was starting to get the hang of it.

Let's try this now. I used my abdomen to lift my torso in one fell swoop, regretting my decision as a rush of dizziness washed over me. I closed my eyes and focused on my breathing until it passed. I turned my head and looked around the room. It was very basic to me, but it would be a scientific anomaly here on Earth. The room was completely white, with no floors or walls visible. The only objects visible were the surgical pod I sat in and the other one about six feet away, connected with various tubes and cords. They appeared as though they were floating in the open space.

I tried to stand up within the pod, but unused to my weight, I slipped and fell out of it. I flinched for the fall with the muscle memory built into my new body, but as there wasn't a floor to fall onto, I just landed in the blank white space, floating between the two pods.

When I tried again to stand up, I placed my foot down, and the ship created a solid yet invisible floor beneath me. I used my hand to push myself off the ground and held my arms out as I stood up—for balance.

This whole experience was new to me, as was everything else. This wasn't the first time my species had to jump ship and head to another planet, but it *was* the first time I was around for it. I was young—about thirty years old in Earth years—and my species can live an abnormally long time thanks to our technological advancements, most notably, our ability to grow and design *any* species of life. We discovered material on our planet that, to put it simply, can be shaped with customized DNA or genetic codes. Using this, we can create clones of anything. Pair this with our groundbreaking discovery of precisely *what* consciousness is and our ability to transfer it from brain to brain, and we can make any body we want and put ourselves inside it. That's what these surgical pods on my ship are for and what they've been doing over the past day or so.

I came to this planet as my own was dying. I found a human specimen, took their body, copied their genetic code, altered the DNA makeup of my current body, and have become them. To make the replacement easier, I also used her brain, copied her memories, and infused them with my own. That way, I can take her place on Earth with ease. I would go down there, live her life for a short while, drift away from her friends and family naturally, and meet up with more of my own that have come here. At least, that was the plan.

One step at a time, I walked toward the other pod, where she lay still inside. I commanded my ship to open the pod and watched as it did.

"Samantha," I said. The vibrations in my throat and the volume of my voice scared me when I heard it for the first time. Samantha, the real one, was asleep—a medically induced coma, as humans would say. I rubbed one hand across the cold, soft skin of her face and rubbed my own face with the other hand. *They feel the same.* I ran my fingers through her black hair. I grabbed my hair from behind my neck and pulled it around to the front. I bent down to hold my hair to hers and compared the two. *Completely identical!* The transformation worked even better than I expected. I analyzed her body further, tracing my fingers down her stomach and hip bones. I followed the same path on my own body, looking for inconsistencies, and I couldn't find any. I noticed a small brown mark near the back of her thigh, just below her butt. I raised her leg to get a better angle of it, twisted my hips around, and found the exact same dot in the exact same spot. *Impressive.* I closed the door to her pod and watched through the glass as the frosty, cold air necessary to preserve her body filled the space. If anything should happen to my body, I would need hers to make me another one.

I commanded my ship to get rid of the bright light that filled the room, and once it faded, the room was completely transparent. I could see the city below as we floated above it.

This is where I've lived my whole life. I tried getting used to that thought, as Samantha's memories were still being mixed with my own. I didn't enjoy it, as I didn't feel like myself anymore. I felt like an intruder. But I didn't have another choice. I had to live this life before I could get back to my own. I scanned the town and tried to recognize all of the locations. If this were something I would commit to, I had to give it my all. The first place I recognized was my high school; I had graduated just last year. I wasn't a big fan of the place, yet almost all of my best memories (Samantha's memories) originated there. It felt unreal, as immersed as I now was in this girl's life, but it felt natural.

The next place I noticed was an apartment complex, Sean's apartment complex.

Poor guy. I wonder how he's doing. Letting curiosity get the better of me, I told my ship to fly toward the complex. I wasn't worried that anybody would see me because I knew they couldn't.

As humans know it, the universe is a lot more complex than they realize. It is divided into multiple levels that I will call planes, and human beings can only perceive and interact with other things on the same plane as they are. Thanks to my species' technological advancements, we can travel outside the usual plane and enter another one. This other plane is an empty void that, while in it, we can still see what is in the usual plane. However, we would fall infinitely into the void of nothing. With my ship constantly resting in this other plane, we can travel discreetly across the universe, stepping in and out of what is perceivable by others as we see fit. Simply put, when on this plane, someone outside cannot see into it, but we can still see them. Another bonus was that we could fly straight through objects, and nothing would ever touch us. It was as if we weren't even there.

I took the ship inside the complex and straight into Sean's apartment. I looked around the inside, walking as if I were actually there, but the ship was really just fabricating a floor that matched the apartment's interior. I checked each room, and there was no sign of Sean, only his less-than-likable roommate, Curtis, who sat at his computer reading an article about Samantha's disappearance. I stood beside him, resting my arm on his shoulder, the feeling fabricated just as much as the floor beneath my heels. I read the article until I got to the part that said Sean had been arrested for the disappearance.

No, not him. I felt sorrow for him, as if the grief came straight from Samantha's brain. I knew I needed to return as Samantha soon to get Sean out of that trouble. I started by commanding the ship back up to the sky, but then I remembered that Emma's apartment was just a few doors down. *How is she handling this?*

I exited Sean's apartment, walking straight through the door as the ship followed me through the halls and built a walkway for me. I entered Emma's apartment the same way I left Sean's. Upon entering, I felt a wave of disorientation rush over me. My eyes struggled to focus on anything, and my feet felt off balance. It didn't last long, and I assumed it was just my body getting used to its new shape. I blinked until my vision cleared. Once I could see again, Emma stood in her kitchen to the right of the entrance, pouring herself a glass of wine.

I watched as she popped pills from her hand into her mouth and washed them down with her wine. It reminded me of the depression meds I (or Samantha) took yesterday morning before the date. My species never needed mental medication of any sort because all thoughts and feelings we had could be manipulated in a multitude of ways, so I wasn't sure if we had ever considered the ramifications of intertwining a human's brain with our own when that human was on medication such as this. But I knew our species was brilliant, and our scientists would've likely thought this through already, so I shrugged it off. I know now that I should've looked more into this, as everything that happens next might've been avoidable, but oh well.

"Hindsight is always 20/20," as people often say. I turned my worries to the idea that Samantha's disappearance led Emma to pill-popping.

Emma poured another glass of wine and said, "I'll be back for *you*." She walked to her front door, where I still stood, and kicked her shoes off, leaving them haphazard on the floor. Then she walked to her bathroom, where I saw the open bottle of Tylenol on the counter.

That makes me feel better.

I watched her turn on the faucet and test the water. The part of my brain that was Samantha's had forgotten Emma didn't know I could see her, but I was swiftly reminded when she took her top off. I closed my eyes so as not to be invasive. I waited for the sound of her bathroom door closing, but it never came. I opened my eyes again once I heard her TV turn on to my right. Emma sat naked on her couch with her feet on her coffee table. *Put some clothes on, girl!* I couldn't blame her, though. She didn't know I was there with her, and it wasn't like we hadn't seen each other like this before. But it did remind me that I wasn't wearing anything, either. Where I came from, nudity was a nonissue. We had evolved past sexual reproduction and were just growing our children, and air temperature was something that could be moderated. When I came to Earth, I hadn't even considered clothing. Had I known then, I would've abducted Samantha with her clothes still on. (What did I say about hindsight?)

I diverted my eyes from Emma to the TV, where the news anchor mentioned a family that had been murdered in town. *I guess they aren't covering Samantha yet, are they?*

Watching it, my head filled with a blistering pain. I felt angry, but not toward any particular source. The longer I heard the news anchor talk about that family's tragedy, the more my blood boiled. I felt like I had lost control of my body while I stood there, shaking with a directionless hatred.

When Emma turned off the TV and closed her eyes, I fell onto the couch beside her, my ship still simulating the area around me. I sat completely paralyzed at Emma's side, watching her while she napped until I fell asleep myself. The air was filled with steam when I woke up, the bath water roaring from the tub. I sat, still paralyzed for a few minutes, which felt like hours, willing her to wake up and rush to turn it off. What was more alarming than being unable to move my body was the fact that my head moved by itself to follow her with my eyes. I watched as she came back to the living room and grabbed her wine glass, a candle, and some matches.

What's going on with me? Emma's face filled with horror as she saw something outside of my range of view. Whoever controlled my body didn't seem as afraid as my head slowly followed her to the open window, where she looked outside before pulling the curtain shut. When Emma returned to the bathroom, she shut the door, and I remained paralyzed on the couch. My head turned to the black TV screen, where I stared at my dark, blurry reflection until my body moved on its own again. This time, it lifted itself entirely off the couch and stepped ominously toward the TV. My body reached its hand for the power button on the bottom left of the screen, and the electricity in the building started acting up—a result of something (my hand) from this outer plane I rested in, transitioning into the real world. This is the same side effect that the real Samantha experienced when I pulled her out of Sean's Mustang and into my ship. The lights in the apartment flickered until they completely shut off the moment my finger touched the power button. On the screen was a picture of me (or Samantha) beside the headline.

"Local College Student Disappears from Drive-In Movie Theater"

Now they're talking about it. I watched the news (without choice) as they spoke about the disappearance, my body completely ignoring Emma coming out of the bathroom, walking behind us, and turning up the TV volume with the remote.

"It has been well over twenty-four hours now, and there is still no sign of Ms. Samantha Roberts, who mysteriously disappeared just last night," the news reporter said.

BZZZT

My head turned to the bathroom, where Emma had also looked. While my body seemed distracted, I commanded my ship to pull us out of the apartment, back into the sky above the town, and fill the room with white again. I hoped this would give me control of my body again, but I was wrong. I blacked out.

When I woke up, I felt cold. My bare body rested atop something hard and dusty. I still couldn't control myself, not even enough to open my eyes. I heard the voice of someone I thought I recognized.

"Oh, thank God! Dude, I found Samantha."

Who is that?

"I said I fucking found Samantha. I need you to get to the high school and help me."

They found me? Am I off my ship?

"Samantha's in this storage closet by the locker room, and she's fucking naked."

Yeah, that sounds like me.

"Someone will think I raped her if they find me here, but I can't just leave her like this to go get help. I need you to come."

Who is he talking to? He must be on the phone.

"Just be quick, dude. I'm freaking out over here."

My eyes opened. In the darkness of what looked like a storage shed, I recognized the guy on the phone as Kyle, an acquaintance of mine (Samantha's) through Ethan and Adalynn. I didn't know much about him other than the fact that he and Adalynn tiptoed around feelings for each other for *years*. I wasn't ever too close to him myself, avoiding as many interactions with the football team as possible, given bad experiences in the past, but he was one of the nicer ones. He was also around us more often than most of the team.

Quietly, my body stood, walked to the nearby shelf, and grabbed a metal baseball bat resting against it.

What the hell?

Then, I approached Kyle, who rustled through the items on another shelf. He dropped his cell phone he used as a light source between the shelves, and I watched him get his arm stuck in the same crack while he dug for it. I waited for him to turn and see me standing there, hoping he could do something that would let me use my body again, but I had no clue what that would be. Shake me? Wake me up? I don't know. Instead, when he *did* finally look at me, I had my bat raised and brought it down on his arm. I watched in terror as I, out of my control, followed him across the stone floor of this storage shed while he cried and screamed helpless words, somehow worse sounds to hear than that of his shoulder popping out of its socket. I felt disgusted when my bare feet stepped into the slimy trail of blood left on the floor from a cut on his forearm. With his back against the wall, I towered over him. I watched as my shadow across his tear-streaked face raised the baseball bat.

"Adalynn, I'm sorry," he cried.

My bat came down on his head, his body gave out, and he collapsed on his side. I screamed. I didn't think it was real, but I heard it echo in the condensed room, and then I knew I had control again.

Really? You killed my friend and left me here to deal with the mess?

I noticed myself calling Kyle "my friend" and my emotional reaction to his death. Mixing Samantha's memories with my own worked much better than I realized. I rushed to Kyle's side and felt his neck for a pulse (it must have been Samantha's instincts that told me to do so) and looked away from the horror that was his face. I thought I felt a beat, so I knew I had to do something.

Against what would have been best for my goal here on Earth—leaving without being noticed—I used my ship to take Kyle's body (clothing included this time) and get him set up in a pod identical to the one used for my transformation. Inside, his body would be preserved, and he would be kept alive in a comatose state like Samantha is right now while I thought about what to do with him.

I found a bucket and mop in the storage shed and did my best to clean the blood off the floor until I remembered Kyle's phone call. Someone was coming, and they were expecting to find Samantha and Kyle. I put the mop and bucket in the corner, reached under the metal shelf to grab Kyle's phone, turned off the flashlight, and tossed it back under the shelf.

I thought about what my options were, and I settled on a plan. Send Samantha's real body here, and they will think Kyle went to look for help. They will probably think he got in trouble or kidnapped by the same person that took Samantha to begin with (which wouldn't be entirely false), but at least with this story, Samantha could intertwine herself back into society in a way that doesn't raise more questions surrounding her disappearance. The only problem is that there can't be two Samanthas running around the same town. I would need another body.

One problem at a time.

I returned to my ship, brought Samantha down to the shed, and positioned her in the corner I woke up in. I wanted it to be as natural as possible. Then, I returned to my ship and used it as I did in Emma and Sean's apartments to stand inside this shed, in the outer plane and out of sight.

Not long after, Ethan and Adalynn arrived and started helping Samantha, confused about Kyle's whereabouts. It was unfortunate, but there wasn't anything else I could do. For my first bit of good luck in this body, Adalynn brought clothing with her to dress Samantha. It was a weird moment that felt like I was watching a movie starring myself, and it made the part of me that was still Samantha uncomfortable, watching

Ethan handle my naked body, but I appreciated the fact that he looked away as often as he could. While they worked together putting clothes on me (her), I broke through the barrier between planes, reached into her bag, and pulled some of her clothes onto the ship with me. They didn't suspect a thing. I looked at the outfit I had acquired: a red dress, a risqué set of underwear, and high heels that were at least a size too small.

Really, Adalynn?

Out of habit, I exited the storage shed so Ethan couldn't see me while I got dressed, knowing full well that he couldn't see me either way. I held up the black mesh lingerie set, and Samantha's memories informed me how to put them on. I looked down to ensure I had done so correctly and saw how see-through they were and how tight they looked on me—I was spilling out of both items. The black polka dots didn't help, as they only seemed to cover every part of my breasts that didn't have nipples.

What is even the point?

Then, I held up the red dress and shivered at the thought of fitting into something so figure-hugging. I held my breath, sucked in my stomach, and pulled the strapless dress over my head and below my arms. I couldn't breathe very well, but the dress did shape my figure quite nicely, and the color would've gone perfectly with my lipstick if it hadn't faded by now.

I looked up and saw another familiar face, Coach Bradley of the high school football team. He walked into the storage shed, muttering something I thought nonsensical. I knew they would all take it from there, and it would be best for me to take my leave now and find a new body. I commanded my ship to take me back up and, as I feared, blacked out once more.

This next portion of the story is embarrassing, but it happened, so I'll do my best to speed through it. I woke up in a dark room, the air filled with steam, and my ass wet from the condensation. I was in charge of my body this time, for now, so I opened my eyes. I was on the floor of a shower. I stepped out of the shower and into the locker room, a mirror image of the girl's locker room I remembered from high school.

This must be the boy's room.

I heard a shower running a few stalls from where I was, so I knew I wasn't alone. I walked toward the exit, but the man in the shower heard me. It was Trent. He approached me in what was the most uncomfortable situation Samantha and I had ever experienced. He aggressively threw himself at me, drunk and naked, and tried to force himself on me. I don't want to give that bit any more attention than it deserves, so I'll just skip to my next point.

I lost control of myself again. My hand reached for his penis (the last thing I would've chosen to touch) and squeezed it. Hard. He screamed and fought back as best he could, but whoever controlled my body wasn't having any of it. I pushed my heel into his injured foot and led him to some lockers, where I placed his head in one and repeatedly smashed it until he was dead.

It didn't feel good. It felt horrible, but unlike Kyle, this guy might've deserved it. And just like with Kyle, I regained control of my body immediately after the assault. Given what I knew about Trent, nobody would be looking for him, at least not anytime soon. His parents, maybe, eventually, but I doubt they would be surprised if he just ditched town one day without a word. I commanded my ship to take his lifeless body, put it in a room where I would not see him, and dispose of it one day when I wasn't paying attention.

In an attempt to avoid blacking out and losing control again, I opted out of returning to my ship and chose to take my chances seeing what was going on outside of the locker room. When I stepped out, I saw the giant Ferris wheel and remembered that the county fair was taking place this weekend.

I could've gone with Sean.

The Samantha part of me wished I had integrated back into society sooner, so I would've enjoyed a night like this with Sean. The real me felt terrible that I ripped Samantha from experiencing this herself.

I didn't let myself mope for long because I knew Samantha would be back soon enough, and without an idea of how long I had blacked out, she could've honestly been back with Sean by now. The thought of them coming to the fair briefly crossed my mind, but considering all the questions the police would have concerning her disappearance, I didn't think it likely that she would show up.

For now, my priorities lay with finding a new body. On top of two Samanthas being in the same town, something was clearly wrong with this body, and I needed to get out of it before I lost control again. Unfortunately, it wasn't that easy.

I didn't even black out this time, but my memory of the events is a little blurry. All I know is it happened very fast. Ethan walked across the football field with his phone in his hand and his key chain hanging from his pocket. I approached him quickly and, without missing a beat, unclicked what looked like a Leatherman from his key chain and thrust the knife into the back of his skull.

Unlike the past two attacks, I didn't regain control afterward. I walked away from the scene and entered the fairgrounds. Almost immediately, I spotted Adalynn crying and running for the women's restroom, wearing only one flip-flop.

Why is she crying? There's no way she found Ethan already, right?

Still having no control, my body followed her into the bathroom and the stall, where she vomited profusely. I tried with all my strength to regain control and stop her from being attacked, but I couldn't. I was lucky enough to get the strength to send a command to my ship and had Adalynn abducted and placed in a surgical pod. Then I heard someone enter the bathroom, and I thought I was screwed. They would find me here, blood on my hands and a ruined toilet that broke against Adalynn's skull. Whatever it was that controlled my body didn't care. I exited the stall and noticed Emma splashing water on her face. I didn't know the current situation. Did she know Samantha was back on Earth? Had she seen her since? Did she know where she was? All I knew was that she was probably shocked to see me.

When I stepped out of the bathroom, my body headed back to the football field, where a commotion had started. Ethan's body was now a crime scene, and the strange men in all-black suits surrounded the area, doing their best to keep people away. I watched with a smile on my face, but only fear in my mind of what I'd become. Whoever was in control right now enjoyed what they were doing.

Eventually, I spotted them: Cynthia, Emma, Sean, and Samantha. They were all together and looking at me, except for Emma, who was screaming at the realization that Ethan was the body on the field.

As if it were a game, I walked out of the crowd and back to the fair. I led them to the Hall of Mirrors, its entrance shaped like an alien's head with an open mouth that you walked through to enter. I looked back at Cynthia, Sean, and Samantha, who still chased me. I wanted to be happy, seeing Samantha and Sean together after everything, but the circumstances made it hard to enjoy *anything*. The rest of these memories are even more hazy, as I completely lost control of the body, and my mind was slipping away with it. I toyed with them as they chased me through the Hall of Mirrors, as if whoever was in control knew exactly where the mirrors were and how all the mechanisms worked.

I managed to separate Sean from the group and held him like a hostage with a shard of glass from a mirror I shattered pressed against his throat. My hand stung as I gripped the glass tightly, slicing my palm open. I felt it all, and it sucked, but whoever controlled me didn't seem to mind. When Samantha and Cynthia found me, Samantha screamed Sean's name. He reached up and pulled my hair, which triggered the cascade of my ankle rolling, the heel snapping off my shoe, and me crashing to the floor. Sean tried to jump on top of me but fell straight onto the glass fragment I held.

Cynthia and Samantha rushed to his aid, but I got up and held his weakening body by the head with my thumbs pressed against his eyes, begging for a reason to push them inward.

They backed off with their hands in the air, and that was when Coach Bradley entered the room and shot me in the back of the head.

When that body died from the gunshot, my consciousness was redirected to my ship, where I watched the rest of the events unfold without an actual body to stand in. The police were called, and they carried the body away. Emma drove Cynthia home. The same all-black suited men at the Ethan crime scene offered to escort Sean to the hospital, and a couple of them stayed behind to interview Samantha and Coach Bradley.

I watched as they shot Coach Bradley in cold blood and tried to do the same to Samantha, who ran into the woods. At this point, I've come to the understanding that this group of suited men must be Earth's (or just the United States') secret branch of the military that would deal with a suspected alien crisis.

Feeling so close to Samantha at this point, having literally experienced everything she ever had, I couldn't let her die like this. Despite my comprehension that she could never feel the same after what I (the thing controlling my body) did to terrorize her, and knowing that I abducted and tried to replace her in the first place, I still felt like she was a friend of mine. In that, I knew her better than I've ever known anyone. I saw the men chase her into the woods and get closer with every minute. Doing the only thing I could at that moment, I abducted her.

Notes From the Author

Hello, readers! If you've made it this far, wow. You're awesome. Stick around for just a bit longer and you'll catch some really cool announcements.

The release of this very special hardcover book marks one year since the day I chose to take a chance and dive into this journey that has since changed my life in more way than I ever imagined. Writing wasn't specifically something I was ever interested in, but it has been a thought of mine for a while now. I'm a very impulsive person, and I make a lot of drastic decisions at completely random times, and this whole storytelling thing just happened to be one of those moments.

I was driving home one day; I'm not sure where from, but I remember being right around the corner from my house. I was fed up with the way my life was moving, and I was realizing that I didn't have any clear path in terms of a career. I was brainstorming what I wanted to do with my life—what kind of work I would be comfortable doing that could earn enough money to take care of my family and not hate myself every minute that I'm there. With a background hobby involving video editing, an obsession with horror films, and so many original story ideas of my own I decided that I wanted to be a filmmaker. Then, I asked myself what I would need to make that pipe dream a reality and I decided on a few things: Money, experience, and a story.

Going over that list, I decided that experience and money will only come with time, but a story is something I could come up with *now*.

Then, I thought, what if I publish my stories? They could gain some traction, maybe some small following, and if I'm lucky, earn me the money needed to get that story on the big screen. Fast forward to today; I have since published a total of three books, I'm gaining some traction, and have a small handful of followers, and while it's not a lot, I'm seeing some money come from it. I didn't expect this thing to take off quickly at all—in fact, I didn't expect *anything* to come from this. I thought I would write my story, publish it, and watch it disappear beneath the thousands of other books that others put out every year. But, that didn't happen. My books are floating around, people are *talking* about them, and above all else, there is potential here.

This kind of potential excites me, and rather than writing off this writing experiment as a temporary thing to make do until I get to my *actual* goal of filmmaking, I only want to get better at this. I'm considering these three novellas of mine as practice, and taking all the knowledge I've gained from this process, along with all of the reviews—positive *and* negative—and putting it into a really big project, which I'm working on now, *while* I am going to school for film production.

As for that project, I've mentioned it around before but haven't given much information on it. It's time for that to change. This project will be my first full-length novel, and while it *is* a standalone novel, it will feature some recurring characters that were either in one of my previous *It Came From* books, or are related to those events in some way. The title of the book is: *Summer Camp for Slasher Victims* and has an expected release date of Summer 2024. I started working on this book on January 25th, 2023, and as I am writing this it is currently September 20th, 2023, so about nine months now. I am still on the first draft, and am less than halfway through with it, though I have been working on it at a much slower pace than usual, just about every one of my first drafts for my novellas took me less than four months. I'm not sure why I'm even talking about this, maybe I'm just making a note to myself, but I think it makes a statement in some manner that proves how much more time and effort I am putting into this script that I am genuinely enjoying more than any other thing I've written. If you've read anything of mine and enjoyed it, I promise that this next book will blow your mind. If you didn't like my other works, try this next one out. For my first three novellas, I didn't feel like I was a *real* writer, whatever that means. Having done it for well over a year now, I'm still not sure I'm comfortable calling myself one, but at least I feel like I know my way around telling a story now.

Now for my second announcement, I don't have a release date or a title for the project, but it is already in the works as well. It is a collection of horror short stories with varying themes. For example, a professor of mine had talked about when creating a character, you want that character to already exist as a real person in your mind before you even begin writing the story. That way, the character will be helpful in figuring out the rest of the story, because you will already know their personality and how they would act in certain situations, and how that could push a narrative. A method he mentioned was writing your character's backstory in a journal, but to do it from their perspective as if they were writing their own story in a diary. This can help you develop their voice and personality. I loved the idea, and for *Summer Camp for Slasher Victims*, just about *every* character has a horrifying backstory that deserves to be written! So, in this project I will have a section dedicated to those characters and their backstories. Then, I will have an uncategorized section of various horror short stories I have written over time. Lastly, I will have a section dedicated to the *It Came From* series, including companion stories to the novellas, as well as original cryptid stories with concepts I came up with that I just never had the time to fully develop.

These companion stories will be similar to *It Came From Above: A Retelling!* in that they will provide some insight into the world I built in the respective books. For example: in *It Came From the Woods*, a *lot* of people wanted to know what happened to Bianca. Maybe there will be some answers in here. How about Daniel's mother's chupacabra story? I've already written it. These are just some examples, but it's something to look forward to if you've been following this series.

Now, going back to *It Came From Above: A Retelling!* This was a story I had written, because I wanted to challenge myself and see how well I could write the story in reverse, answer some questions, and breathe some life and purpose into a character that I found rather interesting: the killer. But most importantly, for the third and final announcement, I thought that story would be a good way for me to get readers a little more prepared for the sequel.

Printed in the USA
CPSIA information can be obtained
at www.ICGtesting.com
LVHW052157131023
761049LV00021B/84/J